The Worrisome War of the wHIMSICAL WIZARDS

New & Improved
10% more raunchy bits with 14 full colored illustrations

Whitney Lee Preston
&
NM REED

The Worrisome War of the Whimsical Wizards — NM Reed & WL Preston

The Worrisome War of the Whimsical Wizards

Whitney Lee Preston
&
NM Reed

Released in 2021 as:
The Dueling Wizards of Simpletown

Copyright © 2022 **Tattered Unicorn Publishing**

All rights reserved. No part of this publication may be reproduced, distributed, or transmitted in any form or by any means, including photocopying, recording, or other electronic or mechanical methods, without the prior written permission of the publisher, except in the case of brief quotations embodied in critical reviews and certain other noncommercial uses permitted by copyright law. For permission requests, write to the publisher, addressed "Attention: Book Rights and Permission," at the address below.

Published in the United States of America

www.TatteredUnicornPublishing.com
On social Media by book title or NM Reed author

Tattered Unicorn Publishing
222 West 6th Street
Suite 400, San Pedro, CA,
www.stellarliterary.com

Order Information and Rights Permission:
Quantity sales. Special discounts might be available on quantity purchases by corporations, associations, and others. For details, contact the publisher at the address above.

For Book Rights Adaptation and other Rights Permission. Call us toll-free at 1-888-945-8513 or send us an email at admin@stellarliterary.com.

The Worrisome War of the Whimsical Wizards   NM Reed & WL Preston

The Worrisome War of the Whimsical Wizards
or
The Dueling Wizards of Simpletown

Whitney Lee Preston & NM Reed

A Tale of Fantasy involving two silly Magicians, and a Cunning Plan by their two-faced servant, involving a host a creatures including some mice, two dancing frogs, dragons, shaved baboons and a vibrating stuffy doll with red hair. Not for the faint of heart, nor young of age. Readers, enter at your own mental peril; parents, use caution and parental forbearance.

The entire story is told here. However the magic bedpan was not available for comment.

It is our hope that the reader of these tales shall be entertained.
That these stories shall cause the reader to laugh, to think, and perhaps to cry a little is the most sincere hope of the creator of these tales you now hold.
We hope you, dear reader, enjoy them as much as we enjoyed creating them.
WLP & NMReed

The Worrisome War of the Whimsical Wizards   NM Reed & WL Preston

Editors Foreword

WL Preston's whimsical masterpiece, The Worrisome War of the Whimsical Wizards (also published as The Dueling Wizards of Simpletown by Xlibris and by Stellar) is a Parody of Parity.

As editor I was asked to give a radio interview for its first publisher, Xlibris, and one on the questions has plagued me. The interviewer asked if the story had value as a teaching element or if it was just entertainment. My answer was that the story had more than just slapstick entertainment in that the main characters were improved by their interactions with one another, that the malfeasance planned by the main interlocutor was soon regretted by him.

I have been asking myself that question ever since. And why is this silly story so funny and cathartic? Then it occurred to me that the story is set up in pairs, as are our lives, with pairs of parents and pairs of siblings, which both Preston and I have. The story is WL Preston's way of reflecting on his own life. Of course! The author is always deeper reflected in his characters and story than seems at first.

The characters are characters in his own family. And reflecting his own childhood, Preston may be trying to resolve his urges to rid himself of those characters so he could get on with the dream of enjoying the good things in life without their interference.

Preston grew up in a 50's parent household, controlling, manipulative, punitive, always with the subtext that conformity will result in happiness. The middle child of three big boys, he was the most sensitive of them and his mother's wish for a girl, hence his first name. They were a military family of one working parent and Preston was expected to go into one or the other of the branches of

American military just like both his parents and both his brothers. He joined the Coast Guard hoping to learn to fly a plane, but was thwarted and left disillusioned after he discovered the body of one of his roommates in the closet hung by suicide.

Preston began an advanced degree at a very good local community college, but dropped out unable to study at home because of the distractions of his two parents and two brothers. Preston had not yet realized that he was a "night person" and should have been attending night school. His later becoming a "night person" is probably an adaptation to an intolerable day time home life. He soon found his vocation at an international shipping concern working grave shift manifesting overseas freight hauling. But always he maintains that history would have been his bailiwick, and I agree. The level of his self-taught knowledge of history amazes the listener and his ability to orate in front of large groups for hours on end would have made him a tremendous history professor.

But alas his pairs of life-foes went unchallenged, until he wrote this story, his first, which he was incapable of doing until both parents passed.

This story has probably been sitting in the back of Preston's mind for decades, growing, accumulating minutia, becoming more complex and funny, when finally he began writing it into journals on his long daily commute by public transit to and from work.

Dibble Dobble is Preston himself, and this poor lost character ends up on the threshold of one wizard or the other, and soon ingratiates himself to both by use of a flip mask and a secret passage between the two wizards' lairs deep in the mountain. The two wizards are so strange to him (like his middle class family) that Dibble Dobble soon formulates a plan of deception to destroy them both so he can collect all their magical loot and sell it on the black market so he can live the good life distraction-free.

Hoping to get them to kill each other, he invents a duel pitting pairs of more magical characters that the wizards themselves are directed to conjure. Finally when the third pair of conjured magical creatures threatens to destroys them all, the characters escape mostly intact from the exploding dueling field. But in their sudden flight from a common danger the mask Dibble Dobble had been using to deceive the two wizards falls out of his pocket and is discovered by them, and now they know they have been deceived and they chase Dibble Dobble down. So Preston is afraid that his deceptions all those years as a child will be discovered by his family.

Dibble Dobble was not wearing the mask at the time of the duel because he was playing a third character, the Wizarding Herald, without the mask because his real face neither of the wizards had ever seen before. I believe this character represents Preston as he has become in his adult life, which, mask-less, is unrecognizable to his family. All during his life with them, he felt he had to wear a mask to hide what he felt was his true identity. And now as an adult he might fantasize about revenge, but the baggage of his deceptions follows him to the end.

And in this story as in life, nothing is resolved. And only some of the true meaning of the conflict is exposed at the end of this highly entertaining yet allegorical story.

But back to that interviewer's question. Is the story educational or just entertainment?

When did we forget the true purpose of fiction? Are we so decadent that we have forgotten about myth and fairy tales? And the power of allegory?

In a world where what's called "Reality" is actually fiction in disguise, and reality is fictionalized and then criticized as not being "real enough", fairy tales began being criticized as too foolish or scary.

When did we lose so much of the power of our imagination in our subconscious, which allows our minds to wander new paths and find meaning in stories that reflect the universal elements of the human condition? When stories, our collective inner narrative, began to be sublimated into being denial's bitch.

But if we allow these stories to permeate our prison cells, we might for a moment get a glimpse outside. And maybe that's the key to why.

NMReed 2021

The Worrisome War of the Whimsical Wizards   NM Reed & WL Preston

The Worrisome War of the Whimsical Wizards   NM Reed & WL Preston

Prologue

Kevin woke up with his face in the dust.
Again.
Since he was becoming a young man and no longer a little boy, and although he was still small for his age, he was no longer cute and his favorite antics were becoming no longer cute nor tolerable. It had been so long since anyone had called him by that name he wasn't sure anymore. It would be music to his ears for someone call him anything but punk or thief or rapscallion

He had been on his own for quite a while now, since that argument between a wizard and a dragon had burned his family's home down with his family in it, while he watched from his play area in the nearby woods.

Everyone said there were no such thing as wizards. Or dragons.

But Kevin knew the truth. He had watched them, these magical creatures that supposedly no longer existed as they destroyed his home and family.

And since then he had been wandering, living on his wits and cunning, barely eaking out a living. Eating from rubbish bins, sneaking buns at a bakery, picking the pocket of a slow old man.

But this was it. The last straw. He had to find another way. Getting kicked out of town after town onto his face in the dust was for the birds.

He would have to find another town to live in and prey upon. A simple town with simple gullible folks he could fool and con into allowing him to live there.

But where?

He traveled a while the dusty road and came upon a village outside another town. He watched the roadside tavern with some interest and thought maybe he could go inside and find a mark, one he could steal from or con into buying his breakfast.

Then he saw it. Right there. An old man in dark robes had just entered the tavern. He watched as the old man raised his arm and pulled out a small stick, and with a slight flick of his wrist, everyone in the tavern froze. Absolutely froze. The old man then walked up to the bar, poured himself a drink, drank it down with a flourish and then turned and left the tavern. And as he walked out the swinging door, he raised the small stick again, swish, and everyone began moving about as if nothing had just happened. Kevin knew what this was. Precisely what this was.

And he was sure that he had not only found his new town, but had finally acquired a real mark.

The Worrisome War of the Whimsical Wizards

NM Reed & WL Preston

Chapter ONE

Picture a sparsely populated world of simple times, and even more simple people. Simple farmers with their unexciting crops. Simple builders, with tactical skills that never go farther than stone and wood. Simple dwellings that never get taller than one story. And people who, for the most part, just want to keep their lives as uncomplicated as possible.

But, how could such a world like this exist?

Well, if one looks back into the past of this "Plain mundane world with little imagination", one would see a very different place. In centuries past this world of the drab was anything but!

It was a world dominated by wizards! Magical motions in the realm of the metaphysical where the rule of the day! Teleportation! Transformation! More than mere tricks, there was actual Magic!

Even simple prestidigitation had an element of real magic involved! Card tricks where faces of the cards spoke! Magic ring tricks that would multiply beyond the usual number! And great clockwork creations that employed magic themselves telling all the time of day, the change of the seasons, and any number of other functions that could be built into them by their wizardly creators! Such was the world as it was. And, of course, a time came when those who worked with magic went beyond that which they could control.

And ambitions perverted and became overwhelming.

Soon, wars broke out. A civilization of thousands of years worth of creation was obliterated overnight. Those few who survived were scattered far and wide. Instead of rebuilding, the few survivors chose to live in seclusion. Those who had not chosen the ways of magic, but who had suffered greatly because of its fury, decided to rebuild their world. But they would keep things simple. No magic! No creations of clockwork! No more perverted wizards!

    They tore down what remained of the wizards realms and built up simple homes, simple farms, and freed themselves of the complicated way of life. Such complications had nearly destroyed their world once already, and these survivors were not about to have it all happen again.

Chapter TWO

Time passed. Memories faded. Truth dwindled and fancy grew. And in that time, the secluded workers of magic saw their numbers dwindle.

Each new generation was ever more tempted to live the simple life. Fewer and fewer wanted to have anything to do with magic. Fear of the past was a big factor in this. Stories of the "great cataclysm" became more and more fantastic with each retelling, even the simple magic of illusion was seen as something to be afraid of.

Such is the time that the reader now finds themselves a simple land of simple people dwelling on it. And the last two secluded workers of magic are living alone and in seclusion, without even the knowledge of each other.

And these two simpletons have no clue as to what their futures hold.

First, we have Bartimon Montinair. A friendly old fellow who only wants to do good with his magic.

But like all wizards since "The Great Fall", he has had to rely on a servant to carry out his wishes, to appear in public for him, as well as gather all the needed items for his magical workings. Over the past few centuries, those wizards foolish enough to expose themselves to the simple folk had ended up getting treated to a simple hanging.

Or a simple drowning

Or a simple stoning.

The simple people have never added anything complicated to their means of execution either, but the results were all the same. The foolish magic user ended up as fertilizer for the farmers fields.

And Bartimon Montinair wanted to avoid that at all costs, just as his teacher before him had done.

Bartimon's teacher, the wise and mysterious Whimsy Williams, was the seventh son of a seventh son and had learned all he knew from his fore bearer, Metaphysical Matilda. She apparently had never told Whimsey Williams who *her* teacher had been, but there was some mention of someone named Phred or Shmoe, or something like that.

Bartimon was raised by Whimsy Williams, having been delivered to him by some confused stork-like bird wearing a purple and orange vest, he found life as a wizard to be a joy. Whimsy taught Barimon all that he had learned from Matilda, as well as all that Williams had "discovered" on his own.

Through magic, Whimsy had extended his life more than 500 years. Meta-Matilda had claimed to be over 1000, though Whimsy sometimes doubted this.

Bartimon himself had managed to extend his own existence by nearly 500 years, following the teachings of Whimsy. Once Whimsy Williams felt that he had passed on all that he knew on to Bartimon, he decided to follow the path his own mysterious teacher had taken.

So Whimsy transformed himself into a giant magical looking-bird. Its feathers were like rainbows, it's eyes like sapphires and its beak and talons like diamonds. Whimsy then took to the sky flying off toward the horizon. Bartimon Montinair watched his mentor fly away, a tear falling from his eye as he bade his teacher goodbye with a wave of his hand.

Unwitnessed by Bartimon was Whimsy's fate. Having seen mystical creatures only seldom, the simple people still knew how to deal with things in the simple and effective manner. Using simple slings, they cast a hail of simple stones at the bird named Whimsy, and brought him down from his lofty heights. That evening, Whimsy's bird remains were served on a simple bed of lettuce with a simple apple in his beak.

Chapter THREE

Bartimon knew none of this. He thought of his mentor flying high in the sky. Little did Bartimon know that Metaphysical Matilda had ended her days adorning the simple folks simple hats with her feathers. Cooking mystical creatures was an everyday thing to the simple folk in those days, so Matilda ended up in a simple stew instead.

Bartimon Montinai , 423 years of age, but looking only about 90, one day decided he needed to seek out others of his kind. So, as was his practice, he rang his silver bell to catch the attention of his own singular and trustworthy servant, Dibble.

Now Dibble had been a steadfast and loyal servant to the goodly and the secretive Bartimon Montinair. Or so it seemed to Bartimon.

But Dibble was in fact, a con artist of great cunning who was working for his own future benefit. Slowly, over time, he had won the trust of Bartimon by bringing him the simple essentials of life, food, drink, toothpicks, and wildlife magazines.

As time went on, Dibble was given more involved and complicated services to perform for Bartimon. At this point in the story, Dibble has the foolish Bartimon's complete trust.

And it is here where we truly begin our tale.

Picture a wizard's laboratory, with bottled "this", caged "that", and something in a big cauldron over in the fireplace, bubbling and burbling. Bartimon Montinair is dressed in light, floor-length robes with the usual array of stars and crescent moons embroidered on them in some material that might have once been dark midnight sky blue. He wears a pointy wizard's hat, similar in color to his robes, with similar faded adornments. The silver bell he has just rung is a work of fine creation, having been crafted by the great "what's-his-name", the mentor of Metaphysical Matilda. And its chime can be heard echoing through the entire stone building where Bartimon dwells in seclusion.

His cave has 53 1/2 rooms, a half being a janitor's closet that Dibble resides in.

The Worrisome War of the Whimsical Wizards — NM Reed & WL Preston

"The cave has 53 1/2 rooms, a half being a janitor's closet that Dibble resides in."

Dibble was just completing his checklist of items he planned to steal and then sell from Bartimon's hoard of goods, when that damnable chime once again set his teeth to rattling. Moving quickly out of his closet, Dibble stuffed his "parchment of purloined pickings" into a convenient pouch on his belt. With the simple clothes of the simple folk covering his small frame, Dibble looked much like one of the simple folk of the surrounding countryside.

The only thing that sets him apart was the addition of an interesting mask he had found outside the hidden dwelling of his master, Bartimon, on that very first day. It looked to be the sort of mask one might wear upon the stage of some Elizabethan play.

With its circular shape, and pointy nose in the center, Dibble decided he would disguise his features, thus giving himself a mysterious air. Below the pointy nose was a grinning mouth while above where the uplifted eyebrows, showing a face of great delight.

Chapter FOUR

Dibble remembered that first day he became servant to wizards.

No sooner had Dibble put on this mask while walking outside Granite Mountain that first day, he was then grabbed by a curiously robed individual by the name of Bartimon Montinair.

Fearing for his life, Dibble quickly explained that he was a simple traveler looking for simple work. Bartimon asked him why he wore a mask. Dibble explained that his own face was damaged, and that he could not produce a smile. The mask allowed him the illusion of a smile.

"Illusion?" Bartimon had cried. "Then you are the servant I have sought for these many years! I am Bartimon Montinair! A wizard of great learning! Will you join me and serve as my eyes and ears in the outside world? You already have the gift of illusion. Perhaps I can teach you more magic!?"

Dibble was at first fearful of this worker of magic. He had heard many tales of the world of wizards, and of the great cataclysm that had brought about their fall. He had managed to uncover some small but valuable items left behind by these workers of magic, only to have them confiscated and destroyed by the simple folk.

Dibble thought that he was meant for something better than the "simple life". And this Bartimon person might just be the one to provide that special something. Perhaps many "special somethings".
And his greed quickly overcame his fear.

"Of course My Magical Master! I, Dibble, will be your willing servant and friend!"

Bartimon then showed him the secret passage into his hidden domain, built within the inside of Granite Mountain.

Bartimon gave Dibble the tour of the 53 stone-walled

rooms. 51 of them were stuffed floor to ceiling with collected items of mystical and magical creation, with years of dust coating everything. The remaining two full-sized rooms were Bartimon's own laboratory and the half room that was a janitor's closet.

    Dibble bowed and politely asked where he would be taking up residence. Bartimon opened a wooden door to a half-sized room which contained a small cot, numerous brooms and mops, and a couple of wooden buckets.

    "I am afraid," Bartimon had said, "this will have to do for the time being. In time I have a plan to empty out one or more of the other rooms, but I have yet to find a proper place for all of the magical items contained therein. I hope, goodly servant Dibble, that you can be patient until that time."

    Dibble had said that he could be patient, but that had been 10 years ago, and at this point, Dibble's patience was nearly at an end.

Chapter FIVE

Dibble had jumped up at the chimes sounding, as was stated earlier, and quickly made his way to his master's laboratory, straightening his mask as he went. Feeling his mask and making certain his "smile" was in place, Dibble entered the laboratory of Bartimon, bowing lowly as he entered.

"My Lord and Master, the goodly and kind Bartimon Montinair. What is thy bidding?"

Dibble always tried to make this sound as sincere as possible, while trying to avoid throwing up his lunch in his mask. His master, completely unaware of the put-on, spoke in his usual overly nasal fashion while addressing his servant.

"Dibble my most worthy and trusted servant, I require you to go forth and seek out something for your magical and Mystical Master, that being me." Snicker, Snicker.

Dibble stood up, looked at his master through his mask, and said, "Another journey in search of lost items of wizardly wonder? A pilgrimage to the "Tower of Observance" in search of some Magician's mortal remains? Or perhaps I pop down to the home of the midwife for a warm cup of milk?"

Bartimon shook his head back and forth in the negative, nearly toppling his pointy hat from the top of his gray-haired skull. "No, goodly Dibble, none of these things, though the warm milk does sound rather good at this moment. No, my trusted servant, I have a greater quest that I must send you on. I will require you to find out if there is another wizard such as I. Another magical wizard. I do not wish to be the last of my kind, and I am lonely for the sound of another magician's voice. Go forth, good Dibble, and see what you can find."

Dibble stood silent for a moment, contemplating this

latest revelation. Dibble did, in fact, know right where to find another wizard. But he had kept that knowledge a secret for the past five years, living here with Bartimon.

Unknown to Bartimon Montinair, Dibble had been serving two masters.

Chapter SIX

Thus far, Dibble had been keeping them a secret from one another. Raking in the loot from one wizard in seclusion had not been enough for the cunning Dibble.

While out and about on one of his many errands for Bartimon, Dibble had journeyed to the other side of Granite Mountain. There, he had noticed a similar hidden entrance to a secret wizard's lair.

With his mask in place, Dibble had decided to use a rock to knock on the secret door. For many minutes, there was silence. Then a sound of many bolts being thrown open could be heard coming from within. Then the "secret" door in the mountain slid inward, and Dibble's nose was assailed by the overwhelming smell of rotten eggs.

He fumbled with his mask, choking and coughing as he did.

"Who dares to seek entrance here!?!" came a booming voice from within the mountain domain. Dibble was just getting his mask set upon his face, when a tall and foul-smelling personage dressed in dusty black robes stepped out.

"I am Mathesus Loton! I am the master of all I survey! I am the Lord of all that is mystical and magical!"

The dark robed man stopped his pontificating and looked down at Dibble. "I apologize for the sulfur smell. One of my experiments has gone Kablooie! Now, who are you, and why do you wear a mask with a frowning face?!"

Dibble reached up and noted that he had accidentally put his mask on upside down. His smile was now a look of unhappiness. The smiling mouth was now a down-turned and forlorn brow. His upturned eyebrows were now the down-turned corners of a grim and sorrowful mouth.

And another idea occurred to Dibble.

Summing up this new wizard quickly, dibble

improvised, "My Lord, I wear this mask to cover my unsightly features. My illusion of a forlorn and unhappy nature is only to give praise to your dark and mysterious majesty. Your wizardly wonder of dark dimensions would surely cause one and all to quiver with fright. Oh, if only I could serve such a master as you. Such terror would we strike in the hearts of simple folk everywhere!"

Mathesus Loton had stopped and looked at the diminutive masked man before him. A few moments had passed before Mathesus finally said, "Wow. You're good. I believe I could find a place for someone like you in my organization. Please, come into my secret mountain retreat. Pardon the dust. I turned the last servant into a newt, and he never got better."

Mathesus Loton, Lord of Dark Magic, and, for the most part, a self-styled bad guy, had hired Dibble as his servant.

Mathesus had even given him a name. "Dobble". It reminded Mathesus of "diabolical", which is how he saw himself. And Dibble, now Dobble, went along with this.

Mathesus Loton then gave "Dobble" the tour of his 53 1/2 rooms. The same sort of clutter filled the rooms of Mathesus as were in Bartimon's hidden domain. And before Mathesus could introduce Dobble to his new half-room, Dobble opened the door, noted the same type of small cot and other janitorial clutter and said, "And this, of course, shall be my humble place of dwelling, oh Dark Lord of Doom!"

Mathesus was momentarily taken aback I this, but quickly recovered his composure.

"As a matter of fact," said Mathesus, "it is. It is truly a gifted servant that knows his place and accepts it! You shall do well in my service, Dobble!"

The Worrisome War of the Whimsical Wizards   NM Reed & WL Preston

Then the "secret" door in the mountain slid inward, and Dibble's nose was assailed by the overwhelming smell of rotten eggs."

Chapter SEVEN

Eyeing the collected loot in the many rooms, Dobble bowed low to his second master and said, "Well indeed my Lord."

That had been five years ago, as was mentioned earlier. And now Dibble was being sent to find Dobble's master per Dibble's Master's request of Wizardly companionship.(If that is too confusing, just go back and start the story again.)

Another idea sprung to the sinister mind of Dibble.

"Shall I carry to this yet undiscovered worker of magic some note and some physical token of your esteem, my goodly master?!"

Again, Dibble bowed low and rechecked his mask to make certain it was in the smiling position on his face. Rejoicing that he, indeed, was putting on a happy grin, Dibble stood up and awaited his master's words.

"Perhaps," said Bartimon scratching at his long gray bear on his grizzled chin, "that would be a wonderful idea. I shall dictate to you what to write while I set about finding some trinket for my fellow worker of wonders."

Dibble stood as the wizard selected and unrolled a clean piece of parchment paper for him, and stood ready with a quill pen and ink well. While Bartimon quickly pulled out drawers from various cabinets and searched his laboratory top to bottom for "just the right thing", he began dictating his message to Dibble.

"Oh goodly and greatly needed friend I seek..." dictated Bartimon.

And Dibble wrote, "O ghastly and good for nothing fiend, whose nose I tweak..."

Bartimon said, "To you, O Wondrous One, I send greetings."

Dibble wrote, "To you, O horrendous one, I send curses."

Bartimon continued noisily to search through drawers and cabinets, all the while continuing his dictation to Dibble.

Bartimon said, "If only we could meet face to face. Perchance an exchange of conversation might enlighten us both to no end."

Dibble wrote, "I challenge you to a Wizard's Dual. Perchance a display of Metaphysical Might will bring about your end!"

"Ahah!" Said Bartimon.

"Um?" Said Dibble.

Bartimon had at last found a trinket to send as a token of his esteem. From a golden chain hung an Emerald as big as a fist. Dibble's mouth began to water. He quickly rolled up his parchment and returned the quill to its inkwell. He bowed again, tucking the rolled scroll in his belt.

"I do not know if this is enough of a token. What do you think, Dibble?" Said Bartimon.

"My Goodly Master," said Dibble, "I think the recipient of this "small" token of your well wishes will indeed get the hint."

Bartimon then handed the valuable item into the sweating palms of Dibble. Dibble quickly secured the item in his belt pouch, making a mental note of the drawer the Bartimon had drawn it from. A quick search of that drawer was definitely in Dibble's future plans.

"Go now," said Bartimon. "Fare thee well on your long journey."

Dibble bowed once again, and then quickly ran out of the wizard's laboratory.

Chapter EIGHT

Dibble made his way out of Bartimon Montinair's hidden home, and quickly ran down to the local town of simple folk.

At their simple market Square, Dibble unloaded the valuable trinket upon some simpler traveler who was more than willing to part with his money. Pocketing most of the profits, Dibble then set about buying a suitably insulting item to hand over to his other master, the Dark and Stinky Mathesus Loton.

It did not take him long to find the proper item. Dibble purchased a rather simple form of wooden flute, which he hung from a simple piece of leather cord. He then went to an animal pen in the Market Square where ducks and geese were being kept. Working quickly, Dibble scooped up a goodly amount of duck and goose poo, which he then stuffed into the wooden flute. Dibble then wrapped the poop- filled pipe in the scroll he had transcribed for Bartimon. He then made his way back to the residence of Bartimon Montinair.

Now why, one would ask, would Dibble go back to the secret hideout of his first master? Why wouldn't Dibble journey around to the other side of the mountain to get to the hidden entrance of his second master, Mathesus Loton?

The reason is easy. Five years back, when Mathesus had hired the cunning Dobble, the doofy wizards were unaware of a secret that lay in the half-rooms, the janitor's closet.

Dibble Dobble had, quite by accident, discovered a secret passage that led directly from Bartimon's janitor's closet to the identical but mirrored-image room in the hideout of Mathesus. *That* is why Dibble Dobble was content to stay in the little half room for the last five years.

A short-cut.

So, quickly making his way back from Simpletown, Dibble slowly and carefully made his way back into Bartimon's hideout. He removed his shoes from his feet, and tip-toed past the Wizard's laboratory.

He need not have bothered.

Bartimon had activated some music-producing relic from the magical past. It was currently singing off-color songs off-key. Bartimon was tone deaf after a lab accident a year ago, so he hardly noticed.

Dibble sneaked past the wizard's lab without raising the alarm. He quickly made his way to his closet room. Once inside, he put his simple shoes back on his feet and then turned his mask to its proper 'Dobble' position.

'Dobble' then laid down on his cot, reaching for a hidden lever near his head. Pushing the lever away from himself, a small panel opened in the wall closest to him. The opening was just large enough for Dibble now Dobble to crawl through.

He had used this passage many times over the past five years. Any time one of the wizards would send him out to find some obscure or difficult-to-find item, Dibble Dobble would simply go over to the other wizard's lab and heist the needed item. He would then return to the first wizard's hideout producing the needed item, sometimes getting a bonus to his meager wages.

Both wizards paid well enough, and Bartimon was often very generous with the bonus money.

But Mathesus had a reputation to maintain. He was "Dark Lord goggledy gook". So paying Dibble Dobble any extra was usually not in the cards.

That was all right with Dibble Dobble. If his latest plan worked, after all he lived in both wizards' hideout, all would be soon be *his*. And he could sleep in which ever bedroom he chose, although Dibble Dobble favored Bartimon's cave over Mathesus' cave. Mathesus Loton had this thing about

The Worrisome War of the Whimsical Wizards NM Reed & WL Preston

saving the cobwebs......It gave Dibble Dobble the heebie-jeebies.

Chapter NINE

Dibble, now Dobble, emerged from his half room in Mathesus Loton's hideout. He double checked his frowning mask, then knocked on the door of Mathesus' laboratory.

From inside, Dobble could hear a small shriek followed by the booming thunder of an indoor explosion.

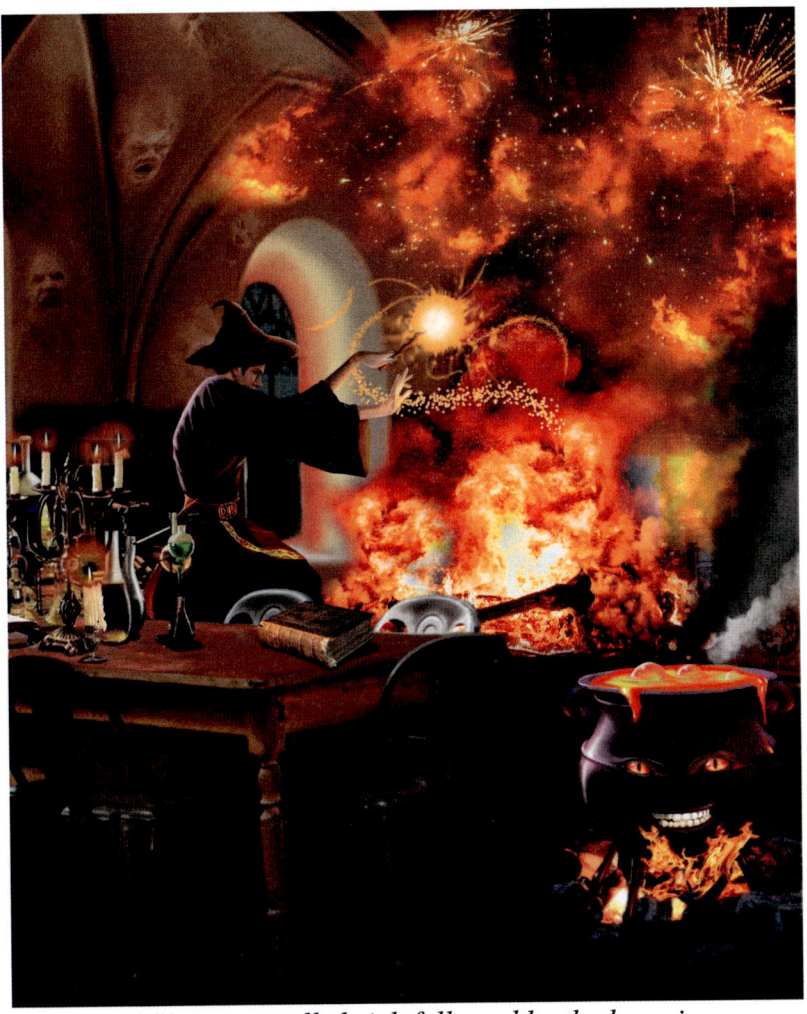

The Worrisome War of the Whimsical Wizards NM Reed & WL Preston

"Dobble could hear a small shriek followed by the booming thunder of an indoor explosion."

After a moment the door was flung open and the dark, towering, and smoking form of of Mathesus Loton walked out. Dobble bowed low, doing his best not to giggle.

"What is the meaning of this intrusion, my lowly lackey?!" Mathesus boomed as he patted out small fires on his robes.

Dobble rose and, without preamble, handed the rolled up scroll to his dark master.

Behind his mask, Dobble was biting his lip, trying to keep from busting out laughing..

Mathesus took the scroll, and slowly began to unroll it. When the first lines of writing were exposed, he stopped and read aloud.

"Oh ghastly fiend," Mathesus then stopped and sniffed the paper. "Goose and duck poop?"

He looked at his servant Dobble, and Dobble felt his bowels move. Was he going to be punished?

Mathesus continued, "This is obviously from some secret admirer of mine. Though a good deal of the writing is unreadable, I think I can barely make out the rest."

Mathesus read on.

"Oh horrendous one." Mathesus stopped again, his dark form exhibiting a curious body language to the eyes of Dobble. Mathesus Loton was getting weak at the knees as he was reading, or rather miss reading, the note crafted by Dobble!

Mathesus said in a voice full of passionate emotion, "a love letter! I have never received such as this! I must read the rest!"

Mathesus unwrapped the last of the poo-besmirched scroll, misreading as he went. "I... You ... A wizards' *duet*. Perchance my metaphysical might will bring you."

To Dibble Dobble's unbelieving eyes, the Dark Lord Mathesus Loton began doing a happy dance!

Dibble Dobble was beginning to doubt his own sanity

while he watched this open display of happiness and joy. A personage of darkness and disaster doing a happy dance?

The poo smeared parchment challenge to a dual, being misread as a love letter?

Dibble Dobble had just about given up hope on another sane moment in his life, when the craziest thing of all happened.

Mathesus Loton picked up Dibble Dobble and kissed him on the lips! Rather, the Dark Lord of Disaster laid a sloppy wet one on the mouth of Dibble Dobble's mask!

This was too much. And Dibble Dobble fainted.

Chapter TEN

Letting his servant's unconscious form carelessly drop from his grasp, Mathesus continued to dance and dance. He made his happy way back into his laboratory, returning a moment later with an ice cold bucket of scummy water. Mathesus then poured this on the unconscious lump that was his servant.

Sputtering and shivering, Dibble Dobble awoke to the sensations of, first, being cold and wet, and second, a bruised tailbone from his fall, and third, getting yelled at by his master, Mathesus Loton.

"Awake, you silly pile of useless flesh! I require you to take this note and this diadem back to my sorceress admirer! She wishes to play a "duet of music" with me? I shall happily oblige! A display of mighty magics, just to impress me?! Hoo rah! Go now, you lowly lackey!"

Dibble Dobble took the rolled parchment and this large, black jewel hanging from a silver chain. As his master danced back into his laboratory, Dibble Dobble crawled slowly back to his janitor's closet. After climbing back onto his cot, he lay back and tried to reconstruct in his mind what had just happened.

He reviewed his careful plan. He had written out the carefully worded challenge from Bartimon to Mathesus. He had sold Bartimon's jewel to some sucker. He had purchased the flute. He had stuffed it with fresh duck and goose poo. He had been wrapped the "poo-pipe" in the scroll.

Suddenly, Dibble Dobble could see his error. The poop had been wet. It had stained some of the words into unreadable blots, leaving a note that somehow Mathesus had interpreted as a love letter from some sorceress!

"This cannot be happening to me," said Dibble Dobble to himself, but out loud. Apparently Mathesus Loton heard his words, for within moments of uttering them, Dibble Dobble was again splashed with cold scummy water from a bucket.

"Get moving, you useless lump! You do not serve the dark Lord by lying around! Make haste! Or I will make waste..... Of **you**!" Mathesus boomed from the hallway.

Dibble Dobble quickly rose from his soaked cot and ran for the exit from master Mathesus' hideout. Once outside, it took a moment for Dibble Dobble's eyes to adjust to the light.

He momentarily wondered at the time of day, then remembered he was on the west side of Granite Mountain. The side of the setting sun. And it just so happened that the sun was doing just that and Dibble Dobble had the realization hit him that night was coming.

And here he was, soaked to the skin with cold water, and having to face a very long walk to the other side of the mountain, because he couldn't go back now and use the hidden short cut. He needed to g all the way back around the mountain to the sunrise side of the mountain in the East. The side with the hideout of the other master, Bartimon Montinair.

Chapter ELEVEN

Dibble Dobble began the long trip, moving as quickly as his legs could carry him. As the day turned into night, Dibble Dobble began to wonder if this "big con" of his was really worth all that he was going through.

He then started wondering about the sound of many padded feet approaching him from behind, and the growling noises that were accompanying the sounds of those feet. In the light of the rising moon, Dibble Dobble turned to see a pack of large wolves running at him. Without any other weapon on his person, Dibble Dobble grabbed the only item in his possession that might give him aid.

The necklace that the dark Lord had given him.

Grabbing it by its chain, he swung the black jewel in an arc in the direction of the advancing pack of wolves.

There was a flash of light from the dark gem, and the pack of charging wolves was suddenly transformed into a group of scurrying mice. Whom quickly fled in all directions.

Dibble Dobble looked with wonder at the black jewel, and then thought again about his "plan of great cunning".

His "big con".

Was it worth it?

"Oh yes it is!" Dibble Dobble said holding this magic gem of creation up to the light of the moon. "It is indeed!"

For some reason the rest of Dibble Dobble's trip was uneventful. Perhaps the other woodland creatures had witnessed what had happened to the large pack of wolves?

Perhaps not.

But Dibble Dobble did not know, nor did he care. He had a usable item of magic, and woe to anything that crossed his path.

As an experiment he waved the black jewel by its chain at a stand of trees. There was another flash of light from the gem, and the trees were now small wooden boxes full of toothpicks. 50 to a box. Dibble Dobble gathered up as many boxes as he could carry. He knew Bartimon would appreciate these.

As Dibble Dobble made his way around Granite Mountain, the big hours of the night started turning into the wee hours of the morning. Predawn light began to replace the waning light of the setting moon. Dibble Dobble could see the village of the simple folk in the distance.

As he stepped onto the travel road that led through the village, Dibble Dobble was suddenly confronted by three rather simple looking bandits. The one standing in the middle was the obvious choice for leader. Biggest build. Biggest club. Biggest scar on the side of his head. And the biggest drooling gap tooth grin as he looked down at Dibble Dobble.

And as far as Dibble Dobble could tell from his own experiences, the worst case of bad breath he had ever run across in all his days.

But the simple bandit leader just had to share it with Dibble Dobble as he spoke. Or more correctly, spat his words at the under-sized servant of wizards.

"Give us your loot!" Said the leader.

"I am sorry gentlemen," replied Dibble Dobble, "but I have no musical instruments today. Perhaps you would like some toothpicks instead?"

"Musical instruments? Toothpicks? I said we want your loot!" said the leader.

"My Lute?" said Dibble Dobble.

"Your loot!" spat the leader.

"As I said, I have no musical instruments. I do have a nice sparkly jewel on a silver chain that the three of you might be interested in. May I show it to you?" said Dibble Dobble, as he did his best to act meek and scared.

The mask still on his face made any facial expressions

he might have made totally unnecessary. And these simple bandits had not commented on it, them being simple and all.

"Bring out the jewel!" spat the leader.

So, once again, Dibble Dobble grabbed the magic gizmo by its chain, and swung it in an arc in front of the simple bandits. There was another flash of light from the jewel, and the three simple bandits became three simple ducklings.

Dibble Dobble noted that one was a particularly ugly duckling, having a scar that ran down the side of his little head. Amidst a great deal of quacking protests, Dibble Dobble gathered up the three ducklings, and took them with him into the Simpletown. At their market Square, he revisited the pen where the ducks and geese were kept. Dibble Dobble then deposited the three duckling bandits into their new home.

"Let us see if you like eating bugs and grain from now on," he said, as the three duck uglies quacked in defiance of him.

Dibble Dobble was really beginning to like his little bauble.

"I wonder what it does to wizards?" thought Dibble Dobble absent-mindedly.

He became determined to find out.

Chapter TWELVE

Dibble Dobble headed out of Simpletown and with the light of a new day at his back, he made his way to Granite Mountain. Once there, he quickly located the secret entrance to Bartimon Montinair's hidden home. Once inside, he made his way to the wizard's laboratory. Dibble Dobble then knocked on the door, awaiting the wizard to open the door.

After a few moments of waiting in the hallway, Dibble Dobble tried to open the door himself. He found it to be locked from the inside. He then listened at the door for the sound of anything going on in the lab. Other than the usual bubbling noises from the big cauldron in the corner, it was quiet in the wizard's laboratory.

Dibble Dobble then crept over to the door of Bartimon's bedroom. Dibble Dobble had only looked in here once before, and the sight had left him with some slightly confused and disturbed feelings about Bartimon.

Seeing that the door was partly open, as usual, Dibble Dobble crept up, as he had crept up last time, and took a peek at his goodly master. He spied Bartimon Montinair in bed, Dibble Dobble was left with a mixed batch of feelings.

The scene of Bartimon's bedroom can be best described as follows: imagine a room with stone walls, ceiling, and floor. Then cover the walls, ceiling, and floor, as well as the inside face of the door, with a thickly woven rug-like material. Imagine all manner of bright colors, in all kinds of interesting patterns, woven into the room-covering material.

Dibble Dobble found that if he gazed too long at the bizarre designs adorning the entire room, his eyes began to cross and his head got dizzy. So he focused in on the wizard's bed in the center of the room.

And what a large and curious sight this was! Picture an enormous bed with a wooden frame, a railing running all the way around, presumably for the safety of the sleeping wizard. But to Dibble Dobble's way of thinking, this was rather odd. It was more like the sort of thing a parent might put a child in. Only much bigger.

And there were other childish flourishes that Dibble Dobble could not fail to notice. The bed was populated by a literal herd of stuffed cloth animal figures, small horses, rabbits, squirrels, frogs, snakes, otters, ferrets, raccoon, bears, and some shaped like people with long orange hair.

Dibble Dobble continued to stare from the doorway. He had absolutely no intention of setting foot inside that room.

The first and only time he had done that, the "herd" of stuffed animals had turned into a "horde". The stuffed playthings had animated magically and attacked Dibble Dobble. They had made a mob attack, moving very quickly, and had overwhelmed the wizard's servant in the doorway to the bedroom.

Dibble Dobble could recall quite clearly being hit, bit, kicked, poked, squeezed, thumped, blown on by a tuba, and pounded mercilessly by the cloth beings of magical creation.

Bartimon Montinair was apparently a very heavy sleeper, because it took several moments of mobbing, and many screams and groans of pain from Dibble Dobble before Bartimon bothered to wake up. More moments passed while Bartimon tried to figure out if he was dreaming or not. His best clue was when one of the orange haired people dolls gave this servant a resounding kick in the cajones.

The high-pitched squeal that came from the throat of Dibble Dobble finally woke the wizard up.

Bartimon Montinair had clapped his hands together and said "sleep my little stuffies! Find slumber my close friends." The mob suddenly fell away from the prone and groaning form of Dibble Dobble, who was wondering at that moment if his family jewels had been turned into worthless heirlooms.

    Bartimon had risen and rushed to the aid of his small servant. After passing his hands in a magical fashion over Dibble Dobble's body the pain in his body began to fade to a dull ache, and finally went away completely.

    Bartimon Montinair had looked down at his vertically challenged servant with a look of great concern on his face.

    Dibble Dobble could recall his words. The wizard had said, "please pardon the overzealous nature of my stuffed friends. Metaphysical Matilda had created them for Whimsy Williams, to comfort him in his sleep, as well as guard him from attack. My mentor Williams had enjoyed them so much, that he made more for himself. A small army in fact. When Whimsy Williams had decided it was time to spread his wings and fly, he bonded his Friends of Cloth to me. Now, they comfort me while I sleep, and protect me from harm. It appears that I will have to do some tinkering with their magic. I need them to accept you as a friend as well. I will need some things from you to make the magic work. First, you will need to remove your mask and let them see your true face."

Chapter THIRTEEN

Dibble Dobble knew that if he did that, revealed himself as the wizard wished, then a possible escape plan of his own devising would be cast into ruin.

Neither of his wizardly employers had actually seen his real face, only his two-faced mask he always wore. Dibble Dobble's plan, should he ever need to employ it, was to take off the mask, strap on some stilts and throw on a long-hooded robe. Then neither of these knuckle-headed wizards would know who he was. Dibble Dobble would then point in some direction and say, in some disguised voice, "Dibble? Dobble? Never heard of him. Check Simpletown nearby. Maybe they know."

So Dibble Dobble's answer to Bartimon asking him to remove his mask had been, "My wizardly lord and master, I thank you, but I must respectfully refuse. It is obvious that such a lowly servant such as I was never meant to tread within the chamber of sleep of such a Grand Wizard as you. I must content myself with my simple servant's dwelling. Thank you for your magic healing of my brutally beaten body, my manhood especially thanks you." And with that Dibble Dobble had saved his plan of escape for another day.

In the here and now, as he stood in the doorway of the wizard's bed chamber, Dibble Dobble winced again at the memory of the attack he had suffered. He entertained the idea of some day getting revenge on those cloth creations of magic. Perhaps several buckets of oil splashed into the bedroom followed by a tossed-in flaming torch. Dibble Dobble especially enjoyed the mental image of that orange-hair doll dancing in the flames. Revenge may be sweet. But pay-back is a total feast.

The Worrisome War of the Whimsical Wizards   NM Reed & WL Preston

"Dibble Dobble looked at the sleeping form of his master Bartimon. As before, the wizard was snuggling several of his stuffed friends with one arm. The other was being used for a different purpose. No, it wasn't under the covers, it was tucked under his chin, holding his thumb securely stuck into his mouth."

Dibble Dobble looked at the sleeping form of his master Bartimon. As before, the wizard was snuggling several of his stuffed friends with one arm. The other was being used for a different purpose. No, it wasn't under the covers, it was tucked under his chin, holding his thumb securely stuck into his mouth.

Dibble Dobble looked down at the black jewel on it's chain, then looked at the helpless wizard, Bartimon Montinair, Dibble Dobble sighed, realizing that he just couldn't do what had just flashed through his mind. He thought he could use the jewel gizmo to change the wizard into something else, something easily squished, but the small servant just did not have the heart. He was a thief after all, not a murderer. He would have to think of something else.

Dibble Dobble glanced down at the small magic gizmo on its silver chain once again. Just then he remembered the scroll message that Mathesus Loton had written. Dibble Dobble held the chain and jewel in one hand, the black jewel dangling free, while he pulled the scroll from his belt with the other hand. And as fate would have it, Bartimon Montinair picked that particular moment to wake up.

Chapter FOURTEEN

"My goodly servant, Dibble," Bartimon said. "Those are for me, I presume? You found the other wizard and he has sent me a note of response? And a token as well! My! A Gem of Transformation! What a gift. My simple token item of Gem Creation falls short of this wonderous item of magic."

Bartimon sat up in bed, leaned forward and took the items from Dibble Dobble's hands. The short servant was thinking of the green jewel on the gold chain that he had sold to some sucker. An item of Gem Creation? Dibble Dobble thought to himself. "Who was the sucker now!" Dibble Dobble muttered to himself.

"What was that, my goodly servant?" asked Bartimon.

"Oh,...nothing, goodly master. What, pray-tell does the note say?"

Bartimon Montinair stood up before Dibble Dobble, his sleeping outfit with button-down flap in back and the footsie pajama legs yet again reminding the small servant that these wizardly types are an odd lot indeed.

A very odd lot.

Bartimon unrolled the scroll and read the words of Mathesus Loton.

"My love!
I will gladly engage in all manner of music making with Thee.
Oh! Such symphonies we shall create.
Oh! Such togetherness we shall enjoy!
Name the time and place of our musical rendezvous and pass the word to my simple servant.
You bring the strings and I shall come to pluck them!
Sighed,
Yours Truly

Of all things Musically, and Eternally,
Mathesus Loton
Dark Master of all things Spooky and Mysterious.
PS Thank you for the token of your appreciation.
It was delicious! "

    Bartimon looked up from the scroll, and stared at Dibble Dobble with something akin to disbelief on his face.
    "This wizard *ATE* the magical token that I sent? Why would he do that? And why is this note written is such an overwhelmingly friendly manner? While I find it wonderful to have such a happy response to a letter of greeting, I am rather confused to the expectations of this other worker of magic. Symphony? Music? What could it possibly mean? And calling me his *love*? Isn't he being just a bit too friendly? What do you think, Dibble?"
    After hearing that Mathesus Loton had eaten the substitute gift that Dibble Dobble had given him, his reply to his master's inquiry was pretty understandable.
    "I think my stomach is making a slow rolling motion over to the left side of my body. Would you excuse me for a moment, goodly master? One of the buckets in the servant's dwelling place is about to receive my fullest and most profound attention. And If I am lucky I will not cough up a lung in the process."
    Dibble Dobble then quickly ran, his gorge quickly rising in his throat, down the hall towards his locker.
    Bartimon, finding the reaction of his servant to the note's wording even more curious than the note itself, did what one might expect a hair-brained wizard to do. He rolled up the scroll, put the silver chain around his neck, and went back to his bed for three more hours of Stuffy snuggles and thumb sucking.
    Bartimon was asleep the instant his head hit his paisley -colored pillow.

Dibble Dobble, on the other hand, was getting through with the rather lengthy process of leaving the contents of his stomach in one of the janitorial buckets. After he was able to get his intestinal processes in some kind of control, Dibble Dobble looked quickly in the bucket making certain that he had not expectorated something vital. Like his liver.

Reassured that he had not spit up any organs, Dibble Dobble laid down on his cot to catch his breath. The moment he closed his eyes, he fell into a very deep sleep. The previous night's journey from the far side of Granite Mountain back to here had definitely caught up with him.

Chapter FIFTEEN

But Dibble Dobble's rest was not to remain untroubled for long. In his mind's eye of the dream world he saw himself walking along in the hall of his other master, the dark and malodorous Mathesus Loton. Dibble Dobble was revisiting an actual event that occurred two years before. But the memory of it still sent shivers down the spine of the small servant in the waking world.

So naturally he had nightmares about it every once in a while.

Like now for instance.

As Dibble Dobble walked through the corridor of his other master, Mathesus Loton, in the dream, his inner mind kept saying, "Nooooo! Don't look in the wizard's bed chamber! Avert your eyes! Turn away! Run! Don't look!"

But, each time, his dream-self kept reliving the moment. Dibble Dobble glanced at the bed chamber door, and saw that it was partly open. He slowly walked up to the entry way, hearing a curious noise, from within, a noise like the sound an angry bee might make, being held prisoner in some glass container.

"Bees, in bed, how curious," thought Dibble Dobble.

He just had to peek in and he wished at that moment that he had been struck blind when he saw what Mathesus Loton had been doing in his bed.

Bees? No.

Something absolutely disgusting. Oh, Yes, indeed!

Where his other master, Bartimon Montinair, had been sucking on his thumb, this more nefarious disgusting master was working on another appendage entirely using a small red-haired doll that seemed to be vibrating loudly..

Did then Dibble Dobble need to visit the janitor's closet to pitch his cookies?

Oh, yes, indeed!

And Quickly!
Oh, the Horror! The Horror!

Dibble Dobble awoke from his terrifying dream, his little body shivering in a cold sweat. A single thought struck his brain like a bolt of lightening.

*These wizards need to kill each other. And **soon**. The pyre is built and the first spark of the tinder box has been struck. It is now time to fan the flames!*

Dibble Dobble quickly rose from his diminutive cot and set about putting on some fresh clothes. He then dug out his set of strap-on stilts, and his long dark hooded robes that he would put on to cover it all. The complete height-enhancing ensemble would put him eye-to-eye with those crazy wizards.

And without his mask on his face, those two old fools would have no idea who he was. Once dressed, he loaded his belt pouches with all the coinage he had collected thus far as earnings as the two wizard's servants. Mixed in there was money he had taken in trade for the gem creation item from Bartimon. Dibble Dobble vowed he would do his best to get that magical item back, if his mark hadn't figured out how to use it yet. If he had, he'd be long gone.

But upon reflection of his luck thus far, Dibble Dobble figured that he had inadvertently made that traveling man a very rich fellow indeed.

But now to the matter at hand.

The wizards. And getting revenge for what the bed-time habits of these two perverts had inflicted on the up-to-now innocent mind of Dibble Dobble.

Chapter SIXTEEN

Dibble Dobble stepped out into the hallway of the strange but goodly wizard Bartimon Montinair's hidden home, with his strap-on stilts, his height-enhancing apparatus, and he made his way to the door of the Wizard's laboratory. Once there, Dibble Dobble rapped loudly upon it, using one of his belt pouches full of coins to add emphasis to his actions. He wanted the wizard to think he was really strong as well as really tall.

And the trick must have worked because Bartimon answered the door immediately.

"Oh," said Bartimon. "I thought you were my servant being rude. Who are you, friend? And how may I be of assistance?" And the old wizard was so doddering that he didn't even consider how this stranger had even gotten *into* his secret lair in the mountain, the front door being hidden and secret and all.

Dibble Dobble just smiled, happy that his mask-less face and his enhanced height had absolutely fooled this knot-headed wizard. He then spoke using his best imitation of Mathesus Loton's voice.

"I am the dark and mysterious servant of my even more dark and mysterious master, Mathesus Loton. Perhaps you've heard of him?" And Dibble Dobble smirked with a sly smile.

"A note and a gift were delivered unto you by your most capable and steadfast servant, the goodly Dibble. My keen and dastardly master requires a reply from you post haste. But as to the place and time of your music-making, he has a suggestion which he arrived at after his parchment was sent with your most grand and wise Dibble."

At this point Dibble Dobble was having a difficult time keeping a straight face, especially troublesome now that it was not hidden by the mask.

Because at that moment Bartimon's face resembled a deer in headlights.

And Dibble Dobble was loving this.

"Dibble, goodly? Yes. Trustworthy? Sure. Steadfast? OK. Grand and Wise? Hmmmm.... I will have to think about that for a time."

Bartimon looked a little more confused than usual. Dibble decided to not be more insulting just yet. Bartimon had treated him fairly well over the years, while Mathesus had used him as a door mat on a number of occasions.

But, no, Dibble Dobble thought. *I must stick to my plan.*

Dibble Dobble cleared his throat loudly to bring Bartimon out of his current road block.

"Oh, yes," said Bartimon, glancing down at the tall and unfamiliar messenger from the other wizard, and he remembered what they had been talking about.

"So, yes, your dark and mysterious master has a most curiously friendly way of sending an invitation to a fellow wizard. And he wishes to meet to form a musical duet? Interesting. I myself," said Bartimon, "have never really appreciated musical arts as much as I should, but I have a clever clockwork device left over from the great times of Wizardry that the Great Mathesus Loton may appreciate. I shall bring it to the appropriate place at the appropriate time."

Dibble Dobble suppressed a smile and a snicker, putting a hand over his mouth and coughing to cover up his sudden merriment.

Bartimon planned on bringing that horrendous sounding *thing* that played off-color songs that were way off-key.

Perfect! Mathesus would want to destroy Bartimon all that much faster. Hurrah!

Dibble Dobble cleared his throat, trying again to contain his happiness. In as deep a voice as he could muster, he spoke again, "That will do quite nicely, no doubt my master will bring an item or several items with which to make music as well. Perhaps you are familiar with the symphony of the angry bee?" Dibble Dobble smiled expansively. "It is one of my master's favorites!"

Bartimon looked confused again. "Oh, I am afraid that piece of music is not one with which I am familiar. Is it one that one might call a "moving" melody?"

Dibble Dobble thought of his expectorating reaction to it, and covered his mouth and began coughing furiously. He almost burst out laughing at this last one.

Once he had himself under control again, he answered, "Yes, Goodly Wizard. That would be an excellent word for it. *Moving.*" He suppressed a giggle and cleared his throat.

"But, now for the time and place! Know you the Tower of Observance?"

Dibble Dobble watched as Bartimon quickly searched his rotten gray matter for the answer to that question.

Several minutes passed as the wizard contemplated the answer his arms crossed in front of him in deep concentration. A couple of times Bartimon looked up at Dibble Dobble pointing his finger as if to say that he knew, then he would shake his head and look back down at his pointy shoes as if to try to jog his dusty memory again.

Dibble Dobble began to lose patience again. "Goodly Wizard!" he said.

"No, wait!" said Bartimon. "I almost had it a moment ago. Just give me a couple more moments to figure this out." The wizard began muttering to himself trying to remember the question to the answer he was trying to find.

Dibble Dobble decided to move this along a little bit faster.

"I am afraid my dark and mysterious master is not a patient man. He does in fact have the patience of a boiling teapot. Mathesus Loton wishes to make music with you as soon as possible. The Tower of Observance is in the middle of the Blasted Plain, remember. The place where the workers of magic used to go to learn, teach, create, and in some cases destroy. Now, do you recall, Good wizard?"

Dibble Dobble anticipated another uncomprehending stare from the wizard. But Bartimon Montinair surprised him.

"The place of Dueling? Why would your master want to make music in such a lifeless place as that?"

Dibble Dobble quickly answered, "I do not question my master as to his dark and mysterious way of doing things. I simply accept it all and move on. And speaking of moving on, the time shall be two days from now, at Dawn. Bring along whatever you feel may be appropriate for the occasion. And I would suggest dressing nicely; that will definitely impress my master. And come alone and leave your servant behind. This magical musical moment must be shared by magicians alone. A wizardly herald will be in the Tower of Observance making certain all is well and above board. Remember your teachings and act accordingly and if all goes well, you two shall make music such as this world has not heard since the Great Fall of the Wizards."

Chapter SEVENTEEN

Dibble Dobble stood as tall as he could in his stilts and robes trying to impress Bartimon Montinair. But the wizard was already making a mental list of all the things that were needed for this trip and his musical moment with another magic caster.

Dibble Dobble took this opportunity to step out of the laboratory. The wizard was so engrossed in his mental workings that the disguised servant's passage was not even noticed.

Dibble Dobble quickly headed to his servant's quarters. And once inside, with the door closed, he rapidly got out of his disguise. The strapped-on stilts had begun to make his legs ache.

Once Dibble Dobble was clear of his disguise, he secured it under his cot. Dibble Dobble then redressed himself in his servant's outfit, together with his mask of happy or sad illusion. Before he put the mask on, he noted that a dark set of lip prints were clearly showing on the mouth of the unhappy face. The sloppy wet one that Master Mathesus had blessed him with must have been quite a filthy blessing indeed.

Dibble Dobble breathed a sigh of relief thanking the Fates that he had been wearing his mask. There was no telling what that Wizardly Freak's loving kiss would have done to his actual skin. Dibble Dobble silently vowed to wear long sleeves, long pants, socks, shoes, gloves, a hat and his ever-present mask to insulate himself from Mathesus Loton's dark festering touch from now on.

After altering and adding to his clothing as needed, Dibble Dobble then lay down upon his cot once again. Again he reached up and activated the lever that opened the hidden servant's passage between the two wizards' secret lairs. Once the panel had opened he climbed into the tunnel, crawling toward the home of the dark and mysterious wizard's lair on the other side of the mountain.

While moving through the small tunnel, Dibble Dobble thought about who had originally built the two dwelling places inside Granite Mountain. He presumed they had to have known about each other, the two different dwellers, that is.

But over time, and since the Great Fall, some things just got over-looked, or, as in the case of this hidden passage, had been forgotten about all together. In this respect the Fates had been kind to the likes of ol' Dibble Dobble. Perhaps they would be beneficiant once again., if Dibble Dobble could just get these idiots to just blast each other to bits, all of the hidden treasures hidden in Granite Mountain would then be his for the taking.

Upon exiting the door to his servant's quarters, Dibble Dobble headed straight for the laboratory of Mathesus Loton. As usual the door was closed. Dibble Dobble checked his frowning mask to make sure it was in the correct "Dobble" position, now with blackened lips, then knocked softly on the door.

Chapter EIGHTEEN

Dibble Dobble knocked again on the solid door to Mathesus Loton's laboratory. This time there was no shriek and no explosion. Indeed, there was a passionate gasp of delight accompanied by the buzzing of what sounded like many angry bees.

Dibble Dobble shuddered and took an involuntary step backward away from the door. Something told him to prepare to run away from there at high speed. But before he could act on the impulse, the door to the lab was flung open from within and the Dark and Mysterious Mathesus Loton stepped into the hallway, revealing himself and his latest mystical, magical and perverted experiment involving things best not talked about. Or even thought about for that matter.

Dibble Dobble's hands shot up in reflex action to cover his eyes from this new version of obscene horror that Mathesus was visiting upon him.

Too late! thought Dibble Dobble. *That part of my memory shall remain scarred forever! And I wanted something* nice *in that part of my brain-case! In time the years shall make me drivel drool and even forget my own name. But the terrible memory of what I have just witnessed shall never fade! The image of this disgusting unnatural spectacle shall remain an open wound, weeping pus within my mind.*

Dibble Dobble stopped himself for a moment, and thought, *Hey, that was good. I should write that down somewhere.*

Though temporarily self-minded, Dibble Dobble's ears could still perceive the sound of many angry bees.

"Sting him to death already so we can have done with this disgusting display," Dibble Dobble muttered to himself behind his two hands and his mask.

"What was that, Dobble?" Mathesus yelled at his vertically-challenged servant standing before him in the doorway.

Dibble Dobble quickly moved on. "My Dark and Mysterious Lord, I bring a reply from the music-loving Sorceress", meaning Barimon Montinair but continuing the ruse.

"Two days from now at dawn, she shall meet you at the Blasted Plain that surrounds the Tower of Observance. She suggests that whatever you plan to bring, make it portable by you, and you alone. I am to stay here, per her order. She stated that a wizardly herald shall be in the Tower to oversee the proceedings."

"Oh, grand!" said Mathesus. "I love it when a third party watches. It adds a sense of the theatrical to what naturally, or, unnaturally, occurs while two are, uh, making music."

Dibble Dobble shuddered again and had a sense that Mathesus was standing proudly, imagining the obscene circumstance. Dibble Dobble had not lowered his hands yet from covering his eyes. But from what his Dark and Dastardly master had just said, his stomach was beginning to make that all too familiar roll to the left. And he had to excuse himself quickly.

"Oh!" said Dibble Dobble.
"Oh?" said Mathesus.
"Yes!" said Dibble Dobble.
"Yes?" said Mathesus.
"Indeed I shall," said Dibble Dobble. And with that, Dibble Dobble quickly turned and ran to the janitor's closet.

He knew his way blind-folded so he did not take his hands away from his eyes. He did not wish to have his sanity damaged twice in one day. *Once was enough, thank you very much!*

In fact when reviewing the visions that were the dark

and disgusting existence of Mathesus Loton's, once was often *waaay* too much.

Page NINETEEN

Dibble Dobble finally took his hands from his eyes, opened the door to his economically-sized servant's quarters, rushed inside and slammed the door behind him. He headed for his favorite bucket and wasted another perfectly good meal, thanks to that perverted prestidigitator Mathesus Loton.

After creating another rainbow out of his mouth, and nose, Dibble Dobble sat back to catch his breath. *I am certain,* thought Dibble Dobble, t*hat a kidney stone passed through my left nostril just then.*

After a few moments rest, the scheming little wizard's servant gathered what meager provisions he had stashed in his dwelling place, and made ready to head back to Bartimon's side of the mountain.

Dibble Dobble took a moment to stick his head out of the door to the janitor's closet. He wanted to listen for any activity that would indicate what Mathesus Loton was doing, if he making ready for his journey to his appointed place of his fictitious music-making with the fictitious "sorceress".

Dibble Dobble caught the distinctive sound of many angry bees buzzing, and the unmistakable noise of his master giggling with perverted glee.

Oh! thought Dibble Dobble, *I look forward to the day when I can make my bladder gladder all over your ashes you pervert.*

He then closed the door, lay down on his cot, and again moved the secret lever to reveal the secret passage back to Bartimon's lair.

Once Dibble Dobble was through the other hidden entrance to the passage, he moved the identical lever back to it's "closed" position. The small passage was hidden once again. Dibble Dobble then turned his mask to display the happy face with the dark lip prints now on the eyebrows, he then headed to Bartimon Montinair's laboratory.

As he approached, he noticed a very curious sight near the lab's door. The entire army of Bartimon's stuffies was now in the hallway floor facing the laboratory door. While Dibble watched with a mixture of fascination and horror, the stuffies appeared to be doing some bizarre dance. And the goodly Wizard Bartimon Montinair was standing in the doorway of his laboratory playing a lively tune on his kazoo. And Dibble Dobble noted with some concern that it was actually a catchy tune, and he would no doubt be ear-wormed by it later. He even caught himself tapping his foot and humming along with the tune. A magic Kazoo obviously.

One more item on the list of things to sell, thought Dibble Dobble.

Before becoming over-whelmed with the ever-increasing urge to join in the dance of Bartimon's bed-mates, Dibble Dobble cleared his throat loudly. He then bowed quite low and respectfully and the Wizard stopped playing his tune and the magic dance ceased. So at least that was good.

Then the stuffy mob all turned and looked at him. Dibble Dobble felt the pit of his stomach drop to the floor as they sprang as a mob and attacked him. The stuffy mob attacked Dibble Dobble just as they had before. That was not so good.

And in seconds, Dibble Dobble was once again getting punched, kicked, poked, and prodded and squeezed.

Fortunately Bartimon rushed to his servant's aid.

But not quickly enough. The damnable orange-haired doll managed to kick Dibble Dobble right in the family pride once again. *One more item,* thought Dibble Dobble, *to add to the funeral pyre after these idiot wizards have finished each other off.*

The Worrisome War of the Whimsical Wizards   NM Reed & WL Preston

Chapter TWENTY

Dibble Dobble gently cradled his injured manhood, while Bartimon cleared away the remaining stuffies.

"Oh, my!" said Bartimon. "I am ever so sorry for the attack you have suffered from my loyal stuffies. I just do not understand why they move against you with such ferocity. Its almost as if they perceive you as some kind of enemy to me. How can this be so?"

Bartimon shook his head as he helped Dibble Dobble with healing magics once again.

After passing his hands over the length of his servant's prone body for several moments, the wizard stopped and looked down at the small man. Bartimon had a look of great concern on his face.

"How do you feel?" he asked him.

Dibble Dobble, thanks to Bartimon's mystic whammy, was feeling better, said, "as though the stuffing had been kicked out of me. Goodly Wizard, Bartimon." He gave a weak smile.

To which Bartimon returned with a tooth-revealing grin. "Right, then. Back to work I must go!"

"Work, my lord?" asked Dibble Dobble.

"Rehearsal, actually," said the Wizard.

Dibble Dobble slowly returned himself to a standing position, keeping a worried eye peeled for those horrid stuffies Bartimon had sent back to his bed chambers. The servant could see that he was safe for a moment.

Dibble Dobble momentarily entertained the cloth doll pyre he was planning in the near future. And he decided to double the size into a full-blown bonfire. The flames would be seen for miles. *And that little monster with the orange hair would be dancing with its hair aflame*, thought Dibble Dobble.

Bartimon Montinair walked resolutely back into his

laboratory. Dibble Dobble could hear the sounds of rummaging once more. But this search was different from the last. And the small servant glanced around the doorway very cautiously. He had no desire for another beat-down from any magically enchanted items.

In the center of the lab was a large cloth sack. It sat on the floor. And Dibble Dobble could see that a number of items had been put inside it.

"Musical instruments, Goodly Wizard?" asked Dibble Dobble.

"Why, yes!" said Bartimon. The wizard was searching through drawers and cabinets, every so often stopping to look at something. After a few more moments, the wizard seemed satisfied he had loaded enough stuff of musical nature into the bag.

Bartimon looked at Dibble Dobble and said, "Please be so good as to pick that up and carry it to the entry way to the outside. And do be careful; there are some magically active items in there. Whatever you do, do not open that bag." He said this last warning as he wagged his finger at his servant.

The Wizard then walked out of his lab, heading directly to his sleeping chamber.

Dibble Dobble could hear Bartimon talking to his stuffies. And from what the short servant could hear from the one-sided conversation it reaffirmed in his mind that the sooner these wizardly twits blasted each other to bits, the better.

"My stead-fast and loyal bed-mates," said Bartimon, "my snuggly wuggly huggable friends, whoooo loves you, each and every one? Why, me!! Your little Barti-Wharti Monti-Wanti, that's who!!"

Dibble Dobble resolved to move away from there as quickly as possible. *I need to keep my lunch where it is this time.* For the weird words of the Wizard Bartimon was spewing, and the sickening cutsie way he was uttering them, was causing Dibble Dobble's stomach to do its usual left hand turn.

"Blasted," said Dibble Dobble. "Blasted to pieces! You damaged wizardly freak! And that Dark and Mysterious freak right along side with you. BOTH of you reduced to ant-sized mouthfuls. And I will be right there to pour honey over the remains to insure the ants will gobble you up that much faster."

Chapter TWENTY-ONE

"Freaks! Freaks! Wizardly Freaks!" The small servant ran ranting to the entrance of the Wizard's mountain abode, dragging the bag of musical gizmos behind him. When he got to the front door, Dibble Dobble stopped and made a sudden realization. This cloth bag he had been dragging, stuffed with all manner of this and that by Bartimon, had almost no weight at all to it. In fact, Dibble Dobble lifted the bag that was nearly as tall as he was, and found it to be no heavier than a sack full of feathers.

"How strange," thought the short servant. "I *know* I saw Bartimon load this bag with lots of mystical, magical, musical loot. It *has* to weigh more than this!"

Dibble Dobble contemplated this latest development for a moment. The bag itself was a deep purple color with a golden colored cord tied at its opening. There was some kind of embroidered message on the outside of it, and its was faded and difficult to read. "CROW ROYA" was all that Dibble Dobble could make out.

He thought for a moment longer. The wizard had warned him to not open the bag. But, why?

What would be the harm in taking a quick peek at the bunch of stuff that would soon belong to him anyway?

What harm, indeed.

Dibble Dobble moved the feather-light bag to the exit portal of Granite Mountain. With both his hands he slowly and carefully untied the granny knot the knuckle-headed wizard had tied into the cord.

At the moment the tied knot was freed, Dibble Dobble was instantly reminded of his last encounter with Bartimon's bed-buddies. The entire contents of the large purple bag emptied into the face of Dibble Dobble, knocking him to the floor.

The multitude of musical, magical items then proceeded

to begin a complicated off-key symphony of musical madness all over his body.

The tambourine was beating a steady beat on the back of his head, the drum sticks were beating out a drum roll on his spine, the Kazoo was blowing duck-like notes in one ear and then the other; the trombone, flute and saxophone were blasting notes at him, and beating themselves against the backs of his legs and arms. And then came the mighty tuba. It covered his backside with its huge mouth and blew powerful notes up Dibble Dobble's bum.

The small servant felt certain he felt both ears pop simultaneously.

After several moments of this musical mob attack, the short servant lost consciousness. When next he was awake, he was looking into the concerned face of Bartimon Montinair bending over him.

And the Wizard was doing his usual healing mojo all over Dibble Dobble's body. And by small degrees, the small servant felt better.

"You have no doubt heard about the fate of the curious feline," said Bartimon in a consoling but slightly sarcastic tone of his overly-nasal voice.

Dibble Dobble simply nodded, not quite sure if that simple physical action would cause his head to fall apart. The memory of the blast from the tuba was still echoing in his ears. Bartimon had passed his wizardly hands over the small servant's body twice more, and then slowly helped Dibble Dobble return to a standing position.

This time when he looked into the bedroom and saw the messy bed, Dibble Dobble noted with a sense of relief that the stuffed monstrosities had been returned to a large purple bag with a golden cord, which was then tied securely, holding the top closed.

So he was safe this time. The wizard had done his magic healing stuff again, thought the short servant, and in the process saved my life again.

"Thank you master," said Dibble Dobble. And he meant it this time.

Then he thought of his cunning plan to fool the Wizards, felt guilty and said out loud, "How can I let you go off to get yourself killed, my goodly master? How can I stand by and let Mathesus Loton blow you to bits on the Blasted Plain? I have set things in motion towards something terrible, and now I regret what I have done. How can you find it in your goodly heart to forgive me, Master Bartimon?"

Dibble Dobble was sobbing as he confessed this to the wizard. And, as usual, the harebrained wizard missed the point altogether.

"I think," said Bartimon, "that you need to sleep for a good long time. A good healing sleep to put your mental marbles back where they belong. I am afraid that the stuffy assault you have suffered has caused your gray matter to go all catty-wampus."

"But master!" cried Dibble.

"Sleep," said Bartimon. And the curtain of sleep and dreamless slumber covered Dibble Dobble like a shroud. The small servant knew no more until he awoke two days later.

Chapter TWENTY-TWO

A while later Dibble Dobble found himself on his own cot in the janitor's closet, dressed in a smaller version of Bartimon's sleepwear. Button-down tail flap and footsies included, with the added feature of a cap with bells on it. Dibble Dobble noted much to his surprise, that his mask was still on his face.

Oh, that fool, thought Dibble Dobble. *That poor, trusting old fool.*

The servant had no way of knowing how much time had passed while he slept, but a sudden sense of urgency set him in motion.

He quickly freed himself from the silly sleepwear, and got himself dressed in his usual simple garb. Dibble Dobble then fetched his "dark and mysterious" costume with his strap-on stilts from under his cot. A quick plan of action was forming in his brain, but Dibble Dobble had a sure sense that the fates were about to hit him up-side the head with a curve ball.

The miniature manservant ran towards Bartimon's laboratory. When he reached it, he noticed that the door stood open and the old wizard was nowhere to be seen. Dibble Dobble then turned toward the door of the wizard's bedchamber.

Again, the door stood open, and Bartimon Montinair, along with his army of stuffies made their absence obvious to one and all by not being there.

Dibble Dobble then dashed to the entryway, hopeful he might catch the goodly wizard as he made ready to leave.

No such luck for the small servant.

The wizard, the stuffed Army of Cloth, and the CROW-ROYA bag were all gone from the granite hideout.

"Dash it all! How am I supposed to save this doddering old fool from the certain destruction I have sent him towards!?" yelled Dibble Dobble to no one in particular.

The vertically challenged fellow was momentarily surprised when, from the open door of the lab, the voice of "no one in particular" answered his question.

"Perhaps," said a voice that sounded like it came from the bottom of the darkest tomb, "I can be of some assistance."

Dibble Dobble took a moment to get his heart rate under control, then he slowly stepped back toward the open portal to the wizard's laboratory. When he reached the doorway, Dibble Dobble carefully peered around the edge of the entry way, uncertain as to what to expect next.

He looked around the lab, expecting to see someone, but there was no one in evidence.

Chapter TWENTY-THREE

"Hello?" Dibble Dobble said.

"Hello," said the creepy voice coming from the direction of the gurgling cauldron in the corner.

"Who are you?" Asked the servant.

"As to *who*, no one in particular anymore," said the voice. "As to *what*, now that is difficult to say. As to *where*, I am that which bubbles and gurgles in the cauldron. But keep your curiosity in check, little man. I can assure you that the horrors of Mathesus Loton visited upon your mind are nothing compared to the waking nightmares you shall suffer after taking a goodly gander at the likes of me."

Dibble Dobble was momentarily dumbstruck.

"Mathesus Loton? The horrors? How do you know about all that? Who are you?" as he was standing, remember, inside the laboratory of the other wizard, Bartimon Montinair.

The Thing in the cauldron made a sighing sound, then said, "we covered that territory already, short stuff. As to how I know as much as I do, stop and think. Have you not noticed a cauldron bubbling and gurgling in a corner of the labs of *both* wizards?"

Dibble Dobble stopped and thought for a moment. He had never really thought about the things that were similar about the two wizards laboratories before. He just figured that, like apples and oranges, the wizardly types were the same, and yet different at the same time.

And then it struck him. Dibble Dobble could remember that both wizards kept a large cauldron bubbling in the corners of their labs.

"So," said Dibble Dobble carefully. "You are somehow connected to whatever or whoever is gurgling and bubbling in that other cauldron? Is that it?" The servant was momentarily hopeful, despite the fact that his knees felt like jelly.

"Not exactly yes," said the voice of "no one in particular" in the cauldron, "and not exactly no. I am in both and neither. I am connected between one wizard's dwelling and the other, much like the servant's tunnel that you frequently make use of."

"You know about that too?" asked Dibble Dobble.

"I do. And I know of your plans to have the wizards destroy each other, so that you may reap the rewards of their deaths," said the voice.

"I have had a change of heart," said Dibble Dobble. "I am sorry for what I have set in motion. All I want now is to stop it from happening. Please! Help me! I do not want my goodly master Bartimon Montinair to be blown to bits! He may be a doddering old fool, but he is a good man! Can you help me to save him? Please tell me that you *can*!"

There was a moment of silence while the Cauldron Thing contemplated Dibble Dobble's words. It then asked, "And the wizard Mathesus Loton? What is to become of Mr. Dark and Mysterious?"

Dibble Dobble's response was immediate. "That perverted freak needs to die!"

"Is that entirely fair?" asked the voice. "You were allowed a change of heart by the fates. Do you not believe that a sordid miscreant like Mathesus Loton can turn over a new leaf?"

"Sordid miscreant? Then you agree that Mathesus Loton is a prime example to all of what is strickly forbidden and why?" said Dibble Dobble.

"Say!" said the voice. "That's good! You should write that down! As to the curious and dastardly nature of the wizard Mathesus, imagine yourself stuck in a magical cauldron with a sexual deviant as an owner. Oh, the horror!"

"But let us not forget the wizard Bartimon," continued the

Thing in the Couldron. "That doddering doofus has dumped more half-baked and harebrained potions into me than I care to think about. Imagine a potion that makes pigs sing. It's a waste of your time, and it annoys the pig. "

Dibble Dobble snickered loudly.

"I am glad you find amusement from such silliness as that," said the voice. "But as for me, the charm of it all wore off back when Metaphysical Matilda made her infamous "talking rock" potion. That bit of magical stupidity ended up getting spilled all over the walls, floors, and ceilings of what is now Bartimon's lair. Ever hear that phrase "If these walls could talk"? Imagine the walls, ceilings and floors having something to say from sunup to sundown, and from nightfall to daybreak. And all of them talking loudly, and all of them at the same time! It took a solid month of Monday's to de-magic that mess! And somewhere during the course of the talking rocks I have no doubt that Meta-Matilda lost her sanity. Why else would she adopt Whimsy Williams to take over for her? You think you have had *issues* with Bartimon? You would have had *archives* with Williams! What a Dingle Doodle that knot-head was! And both of them flying off in the forms of bird brains? How appropriate!" The voice let out a sound similar to a grunt of disgust. But to Dibble Dobble's hearing it sounded more like the gut rumblings of a Dragon. You know, funny and terrifying at the same time.

"You have been around a long time then?" Asked Dibble Dobble.

"Since before the fall of the wizards," said the voice.

"So what can you tell me about what I have to do to stop these two wizards from blasting each other?" Asked Dibble Dobble.

"I have a plan of great cunning in mind," said the voice.

"Oh no," said Dibble Dobble "why does the word "doomed" suddenly spring to mind?"

"You will just have to trust me," said the voice.

"Oh, wait! There's that word *doomed* again," said Dibble Dobble.

"Listen carefully to what I have to say," said the voice.

And Dibble Dobble and the "voice of no one in particular" that did not exist in the two bubbling cauldrons spoke for many moments on the subject of his plan of great cunning. And at the end of their planning session, Dibble Dobble could be heard to say, "Wow. This is going to be a whole lot of fun, but I'm still doomed, right?"

And the voice said, "Probably, but what a way to go!"

Dibble Dobble's knees were feeling like jelly again.

Chapter TWENTY-FOUR

At the Blasted Plain, near the Tower of Observance, three small ducks were seen waddling their way towards the steps of the tower just before dawn. These "duck uglies" had once been three simple bandits. But thanks to Dibble Dobble and a magic gizmo, they were now a trio of total quack ups.

The largest of them, with a scar running down the side of his head, was still smarting from the abuse he had suffered while in the duck and geese pen back in Simpletown. Apparently, three male geese had mistaken the bandit leader for a particularly pretty female goose. After a very heavy session of feathered petting, the bandit chief decided it would be best to leave it once. And when a simple village boy opened the pen to feed the feathered fowl the bandit boss and his two cronies hightailed it out of there.

And they have been the hightailing it ever since.

It seems that ducks are seen as good eating by many creatures in the Woodlands. Their last moment with the Fates had nearly been their end. If it had not been for a doddering old man in weird robes and a pointed hat, the dastardly ducklings would have met their doom.

The ducks had been waddling along, searching for a particular brunt of a human with some sort of magic thingy that had reduced them to their current state of webbed feet and duck bills. The three of them were of one mind about what they intended to do to that short guy, once they caught up with him. Their intentions did not involve anything nice.

After three near misses by hungry woodland creatures, the trio of feather heads were cornered by a large and hungry looking bear. Just when they thought it was all over, they saw a familiar looking flash of light come from some source just behind the bear. The huge bear was suddenly turned into a fat ugly beetle, which the ducks quickly attacked and reduced to three separate duck-sized lunches.

The Worrisome War of the Whimsical Wizards   NM Reed & WL Preston

The ducks had been waddling along, searching for a particular brunt of a human with some sort of magic thingy that had reduced them to their current state of webbed feet and duck bills."

The bandit leader had then looked in the direction of the flash of light, and saw the weirdly dressed man for the first time. The scarface duck and his two cronies recognized the jewel on the silver chain hanging from the old man's neck. It was the same doo hickey that had zapped them earlier changing them from respectable bandits to stupid ducklings.

So after finishing off their beetle bites, they followed along behind the doddering old codger with the purple bag who still had the gemstone hanging from his neck. The old man had saved them from the bear. Perhaps he would return them to their former shapes?

Only time and the fates could tell.

And since the old man was waddling along like a duck, it was not difficult for the three feather brained bandits to keep up with him.

After they followed him for the better part of four hours, the duck trio was beginning to feel rather tired.

Fortunately, the old man was apparently just as fatigued, for he stopped walking, set down his purple bag, and began rummaging around in the sleeves of his robes.

While the three ducks watched from a distance, the old man started to pull out a number of cloth dolls from his robes.

The old man set them down on the ground, forming a circle around himself and his purple bag. When he had completed a full circle with his cloth dolls, the old man then sat down next to the bag. He leaned back and fell asleep immediately.

The duck uglies moved in a bit closer.

The weirdly dressed man was indeed asleep. His snoring sounded like a warthog with a head cold.

The duck bandit chief was still wondering about the cloth dolls that the old man had placed on the ground around him.

The scar faced waterfowl didn't have to wonder for long.

A large snake made its way out of some bushes moving with purpose in the direction of the old man. The snake had just gotten to the ring of cloth dolls when the ducks were suddenly given a curious show of magic in action.

The ring of dolls all animated at the same time and then mob attacked the unsuspecting reptile. Working together, the cloth items of animated magic reduced the snake to something resembling a hat band.

The threat to the old man dealt with, the pet stuffies moved back to their spots in the circle, laid down, and were lifeless once again. The three ducks decided right then and there to follow the old man but at a distance, they had no desire to end up like that snake. So they sat down to wait, taking turns keeping watch.

They moved very little, fearful that another Woodland creature would be sizing them up for a quick but quacking good meal.

Chapter TWENTY-FIVE

Hours passed.
And then night was in full Bloom.
The ducks were soon shown yet another example of enchantment in action.
One of the cloth creations, this one looking like a small woman with long orange hair, stood up and walked over to the old man. The doll first poked, then pulled at the man's clothing.
It was obvious to the ducks that the small magical gizmo was trying to wake up the old man.
After several more attempts were made with no result, the orange haired doll then climbed up on the man's shoulder. From there it was an easy matter of kicking the old man in the head. The loud thunk could be heard some distance away.
This action was met with some success, for the old codger's snoring stopped immediately.
The cloth doll quickly jumped off the old man's shoulder, running and diving back into its position in the circle.
The ducks continued to watch this curious display, as the old man roused himself from his slumbers.
Rubbing his head and glancing around with a confused look on his face, the old man began collecting his cloth creations and returning them to the sleeves of his robes.
He then gathered up his large purple bag, and began walking along again.
The ducks followed, eventually arriving at the place they now were. While they watched from the base of this old disused tower, the old man was witnessed by the ducks to stop and begin preparing for some kind of odd ceremony.
The three quackery's saw the elderly fellow dig out his cloth guardians again. But this time, they were all animated

as soon as he set them down.

The small Army of stuffed dolls formed a protective circle around the old man, while he began untying the Golden cord around the mouth of his purple bag. They watched with some concern as the old person dumped out a pile of musical instruments. The ducks' concerns stemmed from the fact that the musical items were also magic, as they had begun floating around the oddly dressed man. And after a few circular turns around the man, they began to play music.

And, oh, what a noise! The three ducks were debating whether or not to stay and have their small ears assaulted by this magical noise pollution, when they then witnessed another curious sight approaching the tower where they stood.

A dark and mysterious form was moving at high speed across the open, blasted Plain. As it drew nearer, the three duck uglies could just barely make out the shape of the new arrival in the predawn light. It was a man dressed from head to foot in flowing black robes. He was in a seated position, flying along a few feet above the ground, locomotion unknown.

More magic, thought the ducks though they could not initially see what the person in black with seated upon.

In a matter moments, the dark robed individual had flown past the tower, heading rapidly toward the old man and his noise-making band.

This was indeed going to be interesting, thought the three ducks.

The term *interesting* would fall far short of the mark in describing the events that were about to unfold.

PART TWO
Chapter ONE

Bartimon Montinair's journey here to the Tower of Observance had been a rather curious trip indeed.

After tucking his small servant, Dibble, into his bed, with the addition of some proper sleepwear, the wizard had packed up his items and set a course for his current location. The ancient magical Tower of Observance.

The traveling had been easy enough, and he had even managed to save three defenseless ducks that were being attacked by a bear. The Gem of Transformation worked well enough, but Bartimon had hoped to turn the bear into a Crow. His hope was that the bird would then fly away, leaving the ducks in peace.

But when the bear was instead transformed into a beetle, which was then devoured by the trio of ducks, Bartimon had felt regret. He had not intended for the bear to become duck food.

Perhaps the jewel had a flaw in it?

Maybe that was it.

Some time later when he stopped to rest, the wizard had formed a circle around himself and his magic bag with his stuffy guardians. But something must have gotten past his small army of magical cloth creations. He rubbed the large bruise on the side of his head, still trying to figure out what had attacked him there during his sleep. He had noticed a flattened snake near his small camp, the obvious victim of his stuffies.

The sneaky reptile must have been the culprit, thought Bartimon. *And my stuffed friends gave the snake a full measure of their protective wrath!*

Realizing that he needed to travel a bit further, Bartimon had gathered up his cloth friends, picked up his purple bag, and set out to get to the Blasted Plain before the dawn of the new day.

Now here he was at the ancient Tower of Observance on the Blasted Plane.

His stuffies stood around him, awaiting his musical directions on his kazoo. The magical musical instruments were playing a lively tune, although the wizard was rather tone deaf after that explosion in the laboratory last week.

But he was hopeful that he could join his music with the music of this dark and mysterious wizard. This Mathesus Loton.

And speaking of which, thought Bartimon, *who could that be flying towards me at such a high speed? And what manner of flying magical item is that upon which he sits?*

Bartimon Montinair was soon to discover many things, none of which he was going to appreciate at all.

Chapter TWO

Mathesus Loton's short trip to the Blasted Plain had been, thanks to his most prized magical item, easy. His magical enchanted chamber pot. It had many powers, and all of them involved rapid movements.

Very rapid movements. And when he flew along on it, he was often inspired to sing the rhyming song from his childhood:

>Here upon
>a Pot I sit,
>Upon a slotted Pot I sit.

As he had sailed out of his granite hideout, he kept thinking to himself, "Will the sorceress like my creatively cut form-fitted undergarments, with the glow-in-the-dark lace trim?"

Such thoughts filled the sordid brain of the perverted wizard, as he sailed through the air, seated on his magical boom-boom bucket.

As he traveled, he had passed a number of simple farmers, simple villagers, and simple travelers. Mathesus had turned them all into lemmings, and sent them on their way to the nearest cliff.

One particular traveler had caught his interest. The silly sod was wearing a jewel of gem creation. It was green in color, and was hanging from a golden chain. The wizard had taken special care to turn the simple traveler into a fly and then deposit him in the web of a hungry spider. The magical item was then liberated by Mathesus, and it now hung from around his neck.

"I'll paint it black later, so it matches the rest of my matching wardrobe," thought Mathesus Loton.

Chapter THREE

Now here he was, sailing along across the open area of the Blasted Plain. First he spotted the Tower of Observance.

Next, he spotted a person in flowing robes some distance from the tower. There seemed to be a great deal of movement going on around the robed figure. And as the predawn light of the new day revealed a clear image of the person in the distance, Mathesus Loton made a shocking discovery.

"I am wearing sexy underwear, and that is *not* the sorceress I was expecting to abuse."

Dibble Dobble looked out over the Blasted Plain from his official position on the top of the Tower of Observance. He was dressed in his dark, hooded robes, and was wearing his strap-on stilts.

His wardrobe had been at the suggestion of the Voice from the Cauldron. He had brought along one extra item however that the Voice had told him to leave behind. His two-faced mask. Dibble Dobble considered it to be his lucky charm, as it had gotten him out of several scrapes so far. Against the advice of the Voice, Dibble Dobble had it hidden in his robes, certain he may need to use it at some point.

How he had gotten here ahead of the two wizards was still a bit confusing for the small servant's mind. The Voice had instructed him in all that he had to do to keep the two wizards from blasting each other to oblivion. It had then told him to put on his height-enhancing disguise. It then told him to look into a full-length mirror that hung on the wall of Bartimon's lab.

While Dibble Dobble had stood before the reflective glass, the Voice had said:

"To the glass and through

I change your point of view.
There remains so much to do,
to the Tower of Observance go you!"

And as Dibble Dobble had watched, his reflection in the mirror had turned into a view from the top of the high tower. And then, just as suddenly, the small servant was actually there, on top of the Tower of Observance.

Dibble Dobble glanced behind him, seeing the rest of the top of the tower, where a moment before, it had been the lab of Bartimon.

He turned back around and looked, noting the glow of predawn was lighting up the sky. Dibble Dobble could just make out the walking form of what had to be Bartimon Montinair.

Bartimon drew nearer to the tower, and then stopped a short distance away. The short servant watched as Bartimon began to set out his "stuffies", and then to unload his musical instruments. Which were displaying some form of magical animation or another. And it was obvious to Dibble Dobble that his goodly master was still tone deaf, given the horrid noises that were coming from the animated instruments.

Oh, what a disaster in the making, thought Dibble Dobble. Then the small servant's eye was drawn towards a dark shape flying across the Blasted Plain at high speed.

And speaking of disaster, thought Dibble Dobble, *Here he comes riding on his enchanted chamber pot. Oh! The Horror! The Horror!*

Dibble Dobble watched in muted terror as the two wizards faced one another, Mathesus Loton having stopped his forward flight and landing. As the small servant looked on, the dark and mysterious pervert dismounted from his "chamber pot of many rapid motions." There was a loud noise like the sound of a great suction device being

separated from its seal.
"POP!" Sounded the chamber pot.
"Ahhhh!" said Mathesus Loton.
"Ewww!" Said Bartimon Montinair.

Chapter FOUR

"So!" said Mathesus Loton. "We have a small problem. You are *not* the curvaceous sorceress that I had intended to make sweet music with! You are instead some doddering old fool with a questionable taste in fashion, and some magical items. And deactivate your damned noisemakers! You're off-key performance is causing my molars to grind!"

Bartimon made a gesture with both hands, followed by loudly clapping with both hands. The magical musical instruments stopped playing and spinning around the wizard. Slowly they sank to the ground, laying near his "stuffies". The cloth creations still stood around Bartimon, taking an even more defensive stance since the arrival of the dark malodorous magic user.

Dibble Dobble continued to watch from the top of the tower, waiting for just the right moment to act.

Bartimon Montinair cleared his throat, having inhaled a great deal of dust and cheap cologne with the arrival of Mathesus Loton.

"Well," said Bartimon, "you are not exactly what I was expecting either. I was hopeful for an afternoon's musical and magical performance between two wizards of note, no pun intended. You are definitely not the Songbird I was looking forward to singing with."

"And you are definitely not the species of avian I was looking forward to handling. The double-breasted mattress thrasher was more in the line with my aspirations!" shouted Mathesus.

"You ebony bedecked muck mouth!" said Bartimon.

"You Patron of Paisley!" said Mathesus.

"Just what is wrong with Paisley, you grumble-more? I find it to be festive!" said Bartimon, defending his idea of fashion sense. He had dressed in what he had thought to be a colorful array of fine clothes.

Apparently Mathesus had other ideas about fashion. "Festive?!" said Mathesus. "That pattern reminds me of the splatter residue left on the wall after a Dragon has unloaded its stomach contents on a castle! And *that* after eating a particularly badly dressed group of simple villagers! Eyeballs, guts, and earwax included!" said Mathesus.

"You sinister looking snod-grobbler!" Said Bartimon.

"Sinister looking?" said Mathesus, "yes! But snod-grobbler? Only With ketchup!"

"Ketchup!" exclaimed Bartimon. "How rude!"

Mathesus responded, "I have not yet begun to be rude!"

"Murk-mouth!" yelled Bartimon.

"Grumble-more!" spat Mathesus.

"Take that!" called Bartimon, as he made a slapping gesture in the air before his own face. "You fiend!"

Dibble Dobble heard the unmistakable sound of a hard hand slap, and watched Mathesus Loton's head snap back, as if struck by a physical blow.

Mathesus raised a black-gloved hand to his right cheek. He then raised his other hand before himself in a gesture similar to Bartimon's.

"A Slap Spell, you doddering dimwit?" said Mathesus. "I shall answer with the same, but with a different cheek as my target!"

Mathesus made a slapping motion in the air before himself, and Dibble Dobble heard the definite sound of a slap, but this time the noise was somewhat muffled. And Bartimon's physical reaction soon told him why.

Bartimon Montinair reached back with both hands and grabbed one cheek of his behind.

"Oww!" He cried. "That hurt, you villain! My poor hiney!" said Bartimon.

"That," declared Mathesus, "is the first level of abuse

your backside will suffer from me. Have you heard the Song of the Angry Bee? I intend to play a Symphony on the place you sit!"

Chapter FIVE

Dibble Dobble chose that moment to intervene, speaking loudly into a metal cone that the Voice from the Cauldron had supplied him with at the top of the tower.

He repeated the words that the cauldron of Magic had told him. He said, "Workers of Magic!" he announced in his deepest bass the words the Voice had told him. "Followers of the Wizardly Ways! You now stand upon the Blasted Plain! A wizardly Herald watches you from the Tower of Observance! You will abide by the code of conduct as set forth in the Times of Old! What say you?"

There was a stunned silence across the Blasted Plain as all heads turned to listen to the Wizardly Herald at the top of the tower.

The two wizards displayed surprise at first, Bartimon by the look on his face, and Mathesus by his body language. He was masked and hooded as usual, even on the hottest of days. And he smelled like it, too.

Bartimon Montinair was first to respond. "By the edicts of my magician's education, So Say Aye! By the words of my wizardly vows, So Say Aye! And by my promise I pledged to Whimsical William the Wizard, So Say Aye!"

Bartimon then bowed in the direction of the Tower.

Mathesus had a different reply in mind. He turned away from facing the tower, the dark and mysterious wizard dropped his black tights to his knees. He then bent forward and mooned the Tower. "Right in the valley of the Twin Moons, you half-baked nimwit!" Mathesus yelled.

Bartimon took this show of disrespect to the old ways as a personal affront. So much so that he motioned to his stuffy with the orange hair to act.

And it did!

The cloth creation snatched up a musical instrument from the ground and charged forward. And before

Mathesus could stand upright from his mooning position, the orange haired doll cracked him right in the head. A solid blow to the head with a trumpet was heard by all on the Blasted Plain.

And all three ducks and Dibble Dobble winced from the sound of the impact.

They winced even more when Mathesus fell over on his side, landing solidly in the dust and ash on the surface of the Blasted Plain.

The orange haired stuffy was making ready to smack the dark wizard Mathesus in a more personal place below the waist. But Bartimon motioned for it to stop.

The cloth creation complied, grudgingly, dragging the now bent and useless brass instrument behind it. It again took up its defensive position beside Bartimon and awaited his orders. And Dibble Dobble noticed that it was tapping one of its feet as though it were impatient for action.

There will be action soon enough, Dibble Dobble thought to himself, "you little orange-haired monstrosity! And I'm hoping you get destroyed in the cross-fire!"

Dibble Dobble spoke into the metal cone again. "I say again, will the ways of the code be followed? One wizard has spoken in the affirmative. Shall the other respond in the correct manner? Or is another musical beat-down required?"

Mathesus was rubbing his head with one hand, while pulling up his tights with the other. A quick and foul-worded reply had come to mind, but he glanced in the direction of the other wizard, and all of Bartimon's cloth automatons were now armed with musical instruments at this point, and standing ready awaiting the order to attack. The dark and mysterious magician decided to swallow his four-lettered response in favor of something more acceptable.

Mathesus groaned from his position on the ground, "So Say I ! And all that stuff the other guy said...." He then slowly returned himself to a standing position.

Dibble Dobble spoke again, following the script from the Voice of the Cauldron.

"The two wizards shall walk to the tower of Observance. From its base, the wizards shall face outwards. They shall then pace off in opposite directions, stopping when the herald bids them to do so. Now Begin!"

Bartimon Montinair, joined by his cloth creations, walked proudly up to the base of the tower. A number of stuffies made threatening gestures towards Mathesus as they passed by him. He made similar gestures in their direction using the Enchanted Chamber Pot for emphasis.

Dibble Dobble just had to say something before this escalated. "The Dark Wizard shall put his personal Potty away. And the cloth creatures shall be disarmed as well. And all of the musical instruments shall be put away. And may be played by the victorious party after the duel is over."

Reluctantly Mathesus put his magic boom-boom bucket away somewhere in his dark robes.

With an equal reluctance, Bartimon Montinair relieved his stuffies of their musical instruments. The red-haired creation was most difficult, resisting for several moments before Bartimon had to finally deactivate it. The wizard then put the damaged trumpet in the purple bag and stuffed the lifeless stuffy into his sleeve.

The two wizards finally stood at the base of the Tower having kept an eye on each other as they had walked towards it.

Chapter FIVE

The three ducks decided at this point to hide. And they started climbing up the stairs of the tower. The bandit leader of the three duck uglies quacked to his two cronies that he thought that the top of the tower might be a safer place. The two cronies didn't think so. But they never argued with the boss. He might decide to treat them the way the goose had treated *him*. Better to follow, making sure that *he* led the way, of course.

Dibble Dobble first watched as the two wizards stopped at the tower's base, and as they then began to pace off the dueling distance from the Tower. Watching from the top of the tower, Dibble Dobble saw the magicians walk in opposite directions to a certain distance out. He counted their steps silently, then spoke into the metal cone again.

"HOLD!" cried Dibble Dobble. "Hold your positions! Now, turn and face the tower."

Dibble Dobble watched the wizards' reactions as they stopped and turned. As the Voice of the Cauldron had predicted, both of the wizards were put off their guard for just a moment.

Mathesus Loton was naturally the first one to protest. "What kind of crap is this?" he yelled. "How are we supposed to fight a duel when we cant even see each other?"

Bartimon Montinair had similar, but more creatively worded verbiage. "The Babbling Boob in Black does have a point. I must call into question the rules of this battle. How are we to conduct ourselves in this duel if we are to be blind to our opponents location?"

"Simple," said Dibble Dobble, as he followed the script. "This shall be a Duel of Summoning. And each of the wizards shall use their magic power, and call-forth beings described by the herald. The two summoned beings shall then meet at a spot some distance from the Tower where both magicians can view the duel.

"Individual battles between the summoned beings shall be as the herald prescribes. Any cheating by either party shall result in the loss of that round from the guilty party, and awarded to the other wizard. The duel shall go on round by round, until a winner is declared. Do the two wizards understand the tasks before them?"

Dibble Dobble awaited their reply.

Bartimon spoke first. "I understand completely. But may I ask a question?"

"Yes," said Dibble Dobble.

"When a winner is declared, what happens to the loser?" asked Bartimon.

Dibble Dobble followed the script given to him by the Voice of the Cauldron. "At the end, the loser shall surrender all his possessions to the winner. They shall then leave this land and find some place else to dwell."

"Where?" asked Bartimon.

"Far, far, away," said Dibble Dobble.

"And just where might that be?" asked Mathesus Loton.

"The opposite side of the world," said Dibble Dobble, following the script.

"And this has to be a fair fight?" asked Mathesus.

"Yes!" said Dibble Dobble. "The summoned beings shall do battle only as the herald describes. So it shall be done. Are the two combatants ready for their first challenge?"

"So say I !" said Bartimon.

"Ya, whatever," said Mathesus.

Chapter SIX

Now that the two magicians had agreed to the rules, following what the voice had instructed, Dibble Dobble looked for a small wooden box in the space at the of the Tower. He found it next to a set of stairs leading up from within the tower, stairs he hadn't climbed, remember, because he had been magically transported here somehow by the Voice of the Cauldron.

The Box had writing on the lid. "Herald's Magic Tools: only to be used by a herald over-seeing a proper duel. During Improper Duels, the herald is advised to leave the vicinity immediately."

Dibble Dobble opened the wooden box, revealing a set of what had to be magical wands inside. The Voice had told him to select the one marked "Maze" first. It would be used during the first challenge.

From below, the voice of Mathesus could be heard to say, "Any day now, Herald. We are on a time limit after all. The Doddering Dimwit will need his little nappy-poo before too long."

Bartimon replied, "And that bad smell that walks like a man will need his daily potty-training lesson. And his daily beatings."

"Hey!" cried Mathesus. "How did you know about my daily beatings? Have you been using your crystal ball to spy on the goings-on in my bedchamber?"

Bartimon Montinair, Dibble Dobble, the three ducks, and all the active stuffies all went "EEYYWWW" all at the same time.

Dibble Dobble moved quickly to keep the festivities flowing right along. "The wizards shall summon a mouse, one mouse each. The mice shall then race through a maze. The first mouse to cross the finish line is the winner."

"Mouse?" yelled Mathesus.

"Mouse!" cried Dibble Dobble.

"Do we get a choice of its fur color?" asked Mathesus.

"Yes," said Dibble Dobble. "Thought I'm sure your choice will be, let me guess, something of a dark shade."

"Why, yes!" said Mathesus. "Black as midnight, in fact. How did you guess?"

"We wizardly heralds are... hmmmm ... wizards, you know." said Dibble Dobble, getting a bit off-script, but becoming inventive none the less.

"Oh, yes," said Mathesus. "Quite."

"Can I summon a little white one with little gold stars on its fur?" asked Bartimon.

"Why, or course," answered Dibble Dobble.

"Oh, brother," drawled Mathesus with obvious disdain.

"I shall bring forth the maze," said Dibble Dobble. And he pointed the "Maze" wand at a point some distance from the Tower between the two wizards. And he shouted, "Mouse Maze!" per the instructions from the Voice.

And right before their eyes, Dibble Dobble and the two wizards watched a large elaborate maze appear on the blasted Plain.

Chapter SEVEN

The three ducks had not witnessed the magical creation of the mouse maze from their current location on the way up the stairs of the Tower. They were still trying to negotiate the tall stairs built for human legs and feet, not short duck legs with flippers. The stairs led up to the top of the Tower, and the trio of ducks were still busy with their webb-foot duck-climb. They could, on the other hand, or, wing, in this case, hear just fine and knew the duel was about to start.

Then Dibble Dobble made an announcement to the two wizards through the voice cone, speaking in a deep voice.

And he said:

"The two wizards shall now rely on their own individual powers of magic to summon their own mice," said Dibble Dobble following the instructions of the Voice of the Cauldron.

"The place of starting is clearly marked, and the finish line is in the very center of the maze. Looking through the eyes of their mice, the two wizards shall guide their own mouse through the passages of the maze. The first mouse to arrive at the center of the maze is the winner of the first round. We shall then proceed on to round two of the duel."

Bartimon Montinair spoke, "Is there food at the center of the maze? I feel that since I will be calling forth a mouse to serve me in this endeavor, there should be a reward awaiting him at the finish line."

Dibble Dobble was momentarily at a loss as to how to answer this question.

But Mathesus Loton naturally had something snarky to say. "If there is any food at the finish line, *my* mouse will have it all wolfed down by the time your rodent gets there."

"But, you are wrong," cried Bartimon, "mice do not *wolf* their food, they nibble patiently all the while twitching their cute little noses."

Bartimon smiled confidently, obviously certain he had scored a valid point.

Mathesus Loton's response sounded like the noise one might make when one has stepped into a wet pile of something very unpleasant or disgusting.

Dibble Dobble decided to move things right along.

"Goodly wizards," he said. "There will be a reward of food awaiting the winner and the loser. But it shall have to be provided by the magic users themselves, and at the end of the race."

Quick thinking by Dibble Dobble had allowed him to come up with that quick answer to Bartimon's inquiry. It had been outside the scripted routine of the Voice of the Cauldron, but the plucky, small-sized, two-faced servant had learned from his own experiences. Working with these two hair-brained spell-throwers had taught Dibble Dobble to be quick of mind, and fleet of foot as well.

The short fellow-on-stilts adjusted his stance and absentmindedly rubbed his privates with his left hand. The memory of the kicking by that red-haired stuffy was still fresh in his mind. *More fleet of foot and less curiosity of the mind,* thought Dibble Dobble.

Dibble Dobble lifted the speaking cone into his mouth again and said, "The wizards will now summon forth the rodents and begin the race."

"Rat race?" yelled Mathesus.

"Mouse maze for mice," said Dibble Dobble. "Mice only. No rats."

"Of course mice only," said Bartimon. "Mice are nice! Rats are brats!"

Mathesus grumbled. "You are out of luck! You stupid old fu..."

"Gentlemen!" Interrupted Dibble Dobble. "Please let us begin! Summon your mice!"

The Worrisome War of the Whimsical Wizards   NM Reed & WL Preston

Chapter EIGHT

And so, the two wizards began the process of their own versions of a summoning spell. Dibble Dobble observed that the magic workings of Bartimon Montinair were stylish and cute. And, naturally, the magic mumbo-jumbo of Mathesus Loton involved many lewd words and gestures.

Oh, the horrors, thought Dibble Dobble. *I pray to the fates that the mouse he summons is mostly normal.*

And as fate would have it, along with a kick in a sideways direction from Mathesus Loton, the mouse that appeared was "mostly" normal. Other than being deep space black from tip tail to nose, the small rodent was otherwise normal.

And annoyed. *Here we go again,* thought the black mouse. *Once again, I am brought to some weird spot by that even more weird wizard.* The mouse spent a moment inspecting itself. *And he has colored me black once again from front to back. Even my tail ! And my eyes were already black. Why does this mental midget insist on darkening them as well? Again, I can barely see!*

The mouse then looked around at its surroundings. *Oh, lovely!* It thought. *A mouse maze! There had better be some food waiting at the finish line. And it had better be some good food, if I have to put up with this magic mess again!*

The mouse that appeared at the other end of the maze was equally annoyed, especially after it took the time to check out the condition of its fur. *Bartimon!* It thought. *Why must you always do something strange to my fur color?! That paisley pattern last time was revolting! But orange and purple stars on a field of white!? What am I supposed to be now?! A disco mouse!?* The starry mouse looked around at its new surroundings. *Oh good,* it thought. *A mouse maze. That means plenty of tasty food at the finish line, whether I win or not. Bartimon may be a dimwit with no fashion sense, but he has caring and generous to his summoned beasts. Maybe he will give me more of that banana and mango mix! That was yummy enough for me to completely forget about the fur coloring alteration. If, for whatever reason, Bartimon chooses not to give me some goodies to eat after the race, I will just have to make a nest in the middle of one of his "stuffies". Preferably that orange haired little fucker, Zestful.*

    Both mice settled down for the start of the race. They did not have to wait for long. Dibble Dobble raised the metal voice cone to his mouth and said, "GO!"

The Worrisome War of the Whimsical Wizards   NM Reed & WL Preston

Both wizards began to mentally focus on their respective mice. Bartimon could suddenly see through the eyes of his mouse, as well as hear through its ears. And there developed a mental link between the wizard and the rodent. Bartimon sent a mental message to his summoned mouse, *My dear and cute friend, if you can be so good as to make your way through this maze as quickly as you are able, I shall reward you at the finish line.*

The mouse sent a thought back to Bartimon: *Will there be bananas and mangoes like last time?*

Yes my friend. The food shall be waiting for you at the finish line at the center of the maze.

The mouse thought: *Whether I win or lose, right?*

Bartimon answered again, *Yes, my furry friend. Win or lose, you shall be fed well.*

Good, thought the mouse. *It is the least you can do to make up for this bizarre color pattern you put on my fur. Stars? Why stars? Let me guess. They are festive, right?*

Why yes, they are. I am so glad you enjoy them.

The mouse thought back to him, *I did not think that at all, Bartimon. But for the duration of the race and the summoning, I shall endure them. Do I begin now?*

Why yes! Please! Do your best my friend!

And so the star-bedecked mouse started to make his way through the maze, trying to find its center.

On the other side of the maze, things were not going so well between Mathesus Loton and his mouse.

Mathesus! thought the blackened mouse. *You are an idiot!*

That has been said of me time and time again. But I am not bothered. I have a plan of great cunning.

The mouse thought in reply, *You said that last time! And where did I end up!? Playing center stage to something called the greased weasel dance!*

Mathesus answered by thinking, *But you had a great time! You were squealing with delight!*

The mouse thought, *I have news for you, knucklehead. Mice squeal when they are afraid or in pain! Not when they are happy! Only humankind do that glee- filled squealing happy-dance thing! And possibly stupid dragons as well. We rodents are a whole lot more dignified than you two Magic talking monkeys! And why did you darken me from tail tip to nose tip?! I was already black furred.*

Mathesus thought, *Not black enough for me. Now listen closely. I want to spell out my plan.*

The mouse thought, *You can spell? That is news to me.*

Mathesus thought, *All right! Get moving through the maze, you dust bunny with legs!*

The mouse thought, *I can barely see! You darkened my already black eyes as well!*

Mathesus thought, *Oh! That's why looking through your eyes is like looking through smoky glass. Here. Let me fix that.* Poof! *Better?*

The mouse answered, *Yes! Now I can see clearly! So, shall I begin?*

Mathesus snickered. *Yes, but I want you to climb up and over the walls of the maze, heading directly towards the center.*

The response from the darkened rodent was quick, and frantic. *That is cheating. Plain and simple. And I, for one, do not wish to end up getting zapped by some magical trap. Think of something else, Mathesus please!*

But Mathesus Loton was hell bent on a course of action. And since he was generally "hell bent" anyway, there was little chance of anyone changing his mind. Not even a cute, flat-black mouse. *Just do it!* thought the wizard. *I mean to win this dual by any means necessary! Climb, rodent!*

The Worrisome War of the Whimsical Wizards   NM Reed & WL Preston

Chapter NINE

Now, the wizards of old that created the wands that Dibble Dobble was using for the wizards' dual had put a lot of thought into the creation of them.

A whole lot of thought.

They knew, even back in the so-called "enlightened times", that there was always the possibility that some spell-slinger might not play it straight. That someone might try to cheat. So the old wizards put in safeguards to keep the users of the wands, and the parties involved with their effects, safe. They also put in spells that would go off when cheating was detected.

Such as right when the blackened rodent under Mathesus Loton's sway attempted to jump a wall of the mouse maze. A high-voltage shock shield went off and the little mouse screamed.

And to make things really interesting, the wizards of old incorporated empathic spell workings into the anti-cheating effects. Thus, when the dark mouse set off the shock shield, the wizard that summoned it got to feel the full effects as well as the mouse. And that's when Mathesus Loton flopped on his back and started doing a dance referred to as the "dying cockroach".

The black mouse was doing a similar "dance" on the floor of the maze. After the initial *zap* was done surging through the bodies of the two guilty parties, a residual effect was experienced by both the mouse and the spell-caster.

Every hair all over their bodies was standing straight out. For Mathesus, this was concealed by his flowing robes. And this perverted miscreant was actually enjoying the bizarre feeling. The summoned and darkened rodent, on the other hand, was not so fortunate. It resembled a black puffball, and it was not liking this state of affairs one bit.

Mathesus! It thought.

What? thought Mathesus.

You are an idiot! And this proves it ! I warned you, but you did not listen! The total frustrations in the rodent's thoughts was clear enough for even Mathesus Loton's twisted gray matter to understand. But as usual the magic user did not care. He was too busy trying to think up some way to reproduce the truly pleasurable shocking sensation he had just experienced.

Now, if I rewire all of my buzzing bee devices so that their.... The mouse interrupted his train of thought. Derailed it, actually. *Thanks to your brilliant idea about how to win, I am currently in a position where even forward motion is out of the question!* The mouse thought loudly.

What do you mean? Just follow the maze. Cheating is obviously out of the question, though I wouldn't mind getting zapped one more time. That was thrilling!

The mouse responded with, *I would sooner let myself be played with by a group of hungry felines! Besides, I just told you I can't move! My fur is standing out straight, away from my body. My legs can't reach the floor of the maze. I am stuck until this effect wears off! You idiot!*

Hmmm... Thought Mathesus. *I hope it doesn't wear off too soon. I rather enjoy my hair standing out straight. What a new sensation! Say, do you think you could nudge that shock shield just a little bit more for me?* The mental image of the twisted wizard practically drooling at the thought of getting zapped again, began to form in the small rodent's brain. This resulted in the animals stomach doing a slow roll to the left.

You perverted excuse for a wizard! You make me sick! thought the mouse.

Mathesus replied with, *Sticks and stones and sticks and sticks. Beat me right and I'll do tricks. Beat me wrong I'll sing a song. Spew unbacked words, and I'll be gone.!* Give it up, wanna-be rat. *I have either heard and repeated, or made up on my own, all of the worst that language can convey. Now, as soon as you can, get moving. I will be busy for a time, coming up with a variation of the vibrating bed.*

The mouse did its best to block out any more of the images that were spilling like raw sewage from the mind of Mathesus. But it was extremely difficult while the summoning spell was still in effect.

Bartimon and his mouse were having a wonderful little adventure going through the maze. That is, the mouse was doing the footwork, and Bartimon was along for a mental ride, as it were.

Go left! thought Bartimon.

I did that, thought the mouse. *It ended in a dead end! I am going right this time.* The mouse moved forward, turned right, then continued on its way down a different part of the maze.

Hooray! thought Bartimon. *We just might win!*

We will see, thought the mouse. *I am really looking forward to bananas and mangoes.*

Dibble Dobble was watching the progress of the race from the top of the tower. He was not at all surprised that Mathesus tried to have his mouse cheat.

The "Voice of No One In Particular" that spoke from the bubbling cauldron had even warned him that this would happen. Technically, Dibble Dobble could have called a halt to the round, awarding the win to Bartimon. Mathesus had clearly cheated. But it was clear to the small servant that Bartimon and his mouse were having fun. And thanks to the effects of the shock shield, the mouse that Mathesus had summoned would not be going anywhere for several moments anyway.

Let's just see what happens, thought Dibble Dobble.

Chapter TEN

Bartimon and his star-furred white mouse continued to explore the maze, finding many dead ends. The mouse that Mathesus had summoned was still stuck at its starting point.

As time went on, Dibble Dobble began to wonder if Mathesus had lost track of what was going on. The small servant glanced over periodically to check the progress, if any, of the dark wizard and his darkened mouse.

But Mathesus seem to be making notes and scrawling on a scroll, while the mouse was still a puffball and stuck in place.

Dibble Dobble had a feeling that, from his own experiences with the man, Mr. Dark and Mysterious was in a mood of invention, frightening as that was..

And that the results would be, no doubt, something else that was perverted and just plain wrong.

But, Dibble Dobble reasoned, at least it was keeping Mathesus Loton busy, allowing Bartimon Montinair an easy victory in this first challenge.

But Dibble Dobble had momentarily forgoten about the goodly, but addled, mind of Bartimon.

The not-so-simple servant was quickly reminded all too soon.

Bartimon's mouse had explored a great deal of the maze, but was still a good distance from the finish line. The star-decorated mouse made a right turn down another hallway of the maze, and came nose to nose with the black puffball.

Mathesus' mouse was still feeling like a non-mobile sea urchin. He looked up from his solitary musings, and looked at the starpatterned mouse with an expression of surprise. This quickly turned into an expression of utter amazement. The star- bedecked rodent read the look clearly.

"Before you burst out laughing, Ralph," said the star mouse, "you really ought to take a look in the mirror. I can only guess, but I would say that you have all the ear and tale marks of a Mathesus whammy. And your current hairstyle doesn't do much for forward traction, does it?"

The blackened puffball lost his smirking look rapidly. "And here I was thinking you looked silly, Fred," said Ralph.

"I apologize. Any chance you could help a fellow rodent out? Mathesus got me into this mess, then ignored me altogether. I have visions of sewage swirling in my brain, thanks to his use of a summoning spell. He must be coming up with some new invention of a perverse nature."

"You poor rodent," said Fred. "Here. Take hold of my tail. With your hair standing out like that, it should be easy to pull you along behind me." Fred turned around and raised his tail up so Ralph could take a hold of it with his front paws. Fred then started pulling Ralph along through the maze. Bartimon Montinair had been following this exchange between the two mice. At first, he thought it was cute, but he soon found that he needed to raise an objection.

"Ummm..." Bartimon began, addressing the Tower and Dibble Dobble. "Is this legal? What the mice are doing, that is?"

Dibble Dobble was at a loss as to what to say. The "Voice of No One In Particular" from the bubbling cauldron had not briefed him on what to do if something like this happened. Dibble Dobble decided to be inventive. He raised the metal speaking cone to his mouth, and spoke as deeply as his vocal cords would allow.

"There is no rule against the summoned beings giving aid to one another. As long as neither dueling wizard objects, the mice may carry on as they are." Dibble Dobble looked at Bartimon directly. "Being there isn't any objection from the side of the field?"

The orange haired stuffy, who was sticking its head out of one of Bartimon sleeves, shook its head vigorously back and forth in a negative manner. Dibble Dobble watched with glee as Bartimon Montinair grabbed the rebellious stuffy by the head. The wizard then pulled it out of his sleeve, and held it out in front of himself. Bartimon tapped the orange-haired cloth doll right between the eyes and said loudly, "Sleep now my cloth friend!"

But the cloth creation continued to struggle in the wizard's grasp.

Dibble Dobble watched closely, while the goodly spell-caster and his orange haired creation continued to argue. Bartimon was providing the only verbal elements to the battle of wills, while the human-shaped stuffy was making any number of gestures and speaking volumes with body language.

Dibble Dobble was so hopeful that the goodly Bartimon would de-magic the little monster. The short servant absently adjusted his undergarments. Especially in the area of his family jewels. The memory of being kicked there by that orange-haired beast still made him wince. Dibble Dobble continued to watch in amazement as the cloth doll and its owner continued to do battle. He could hear poor Bartimon pleading with his magic creation.

"Please, Zestful! Stop this commotion! You are not to interfere with the goings on in the maze.! There are rules, and they must be obeyed! Please, Zesty, stop your fussing!"

But the orange-haired magic doll would not stop struggling in Bartimon's hands. Dibble Dobble began to wonder if he should say something.

But Mathesus Loton, once again, was the first to offer a suggestion.

"I have a solution to your problem of rebellious cloth creations," as he looked up from his scroll.

Both Bartimon and the rebel stuffy stopped what they were doing, and looked in the direction of Mathesus. Considering their positioning by design, all they could see was the tower. But they could hear the dark wizard clearly.

Bartimon cleared his throat, looked at the problem doll in his hands, then looked in the direction of Mathesus. The orange-haired stuffy doll was still looking in the direction of "Mr. Dark and Mysterious".

"What," said Bartimon, "is your suggestion? It wouldn't be anything naughty, would it? Zestful has been bad, but not *that* ba."

Mathesus replied, looking back down again as he spoke. He was making more notes on his new "invention" scroll. "Let the doll go. Just let it drop. If it chooses to do things as you wish, then so be it. If it chooses to do things as I would, then we shall both be entertained. Let it drop, duffer! Your control over it must have faded. It probably has a mind of its own by now. Do as I bid. Just drop it!"

This last was said loudly, and Mathesus was looking in the direction of the maze. Dibble Dobble could see that the black robe-clad spell-slinger was waiting to see something happen.

He did not have to wait long. Dibble Dobble glanced over in the direction of the goodly wizard, just in time to see the bad-tempered cloth creation pull a dastardly move. The little orange-haired monstrosity gripped one of Bartimon's pinky fingers with both of its little hands. It then twisted that digit until an audible pop was heard by all on the Blasted Plain.

Mathesus yelled from the other end of the playing field, "Pinky finger of the right hand! I would know that sound anywhere!" The dark wizard grinned, anticipating what happened next.

Bartimon screamed.

Loudly.

To Dibble Dobble's ears, and with Bartimon's nasal speech pattern, the noise was like a pig's squeal.

"High C, with a flat E minor undertone. The sound of real pain," yelled Mathesus. "Why not spare yourself some agony? Toss that little freak on the maze!"

And to the surprise of Dibble Dobble, Bartimon did just as Mathesus suggested. Desperate to get the orange-haired torture toy off of his hand, the goodly wizard in paisley flung his arm out toward the maze. The surprised stuffy went sailing through the air, and proceeded to be bounced back into the air by the same shock field that had zapped Ralph the mouse. Apparently the wise old wizards of the past did not want any problems to come *into* the maze from the outside, either.

For the next several moments, every time gravity dragged the cloth creation down to the maze, the shock shield would send it airborne once again.

And with each jolt, orange hair on the head of the stuffy would stand out straight, while the magic doll convulsed with pain.

Dibble Dobble watched in wicked glee as the arch-nemesis of his family jewels finally got *its own*!

Chapter ELEVEN

ZAP! ZAP! ZAP!

"Fry, you toilet bowl rag!" said Dibble Dobble. "You carrot- topped piece of sh.... OWWW!" Yelled Dibble Dobble. The small servant looked down to see what had caused his left ankle to suddenly hurt badly. He was amazed to see three ducks. Two stood side-by-side, while the third stood straddling the others backs. The one on top of the feathered pyramid had just bitten Dibble Dobble in the leg. And the small servant could see a familiar scar on the side of the head of his tormentor.

Without a moment's thought, Dibble Dobble grabbed the stone rail of the tower top with both hands. He then kicked out with all his might, using his stilt -laden leg to its full potential. The three ducks all quacked with rage as they were all sent back down the stairs that they had worked so hard to climb.

Dibble Dobble could hear their quacked curses get fainter and fainter as they continued to tumble all the way back down to the bottom. The small servant made a mental note that, along with the foolish folly of these two wizards, he might just have to make some duck soup.

And suddenly his mouth started watering. Dibble Dobble realized he had not had anything to eat in a while. Maybe a breakfast break was in order.

Lunch. After this first event is over, thought Dibble Dobble.

"Go mice!!" He yelled into the metal speaking cone, trying to hurry them onto some kind of victory. But the stuffed doll with the orange hair was distracting everyone on the field of contest. The shock shield of the maze was still sending it skyward only to have it fall down for another zap.

As Dibble Dobble watched, someone finally took action

for the benefit of the cloth doll. But the small servant had to wonder just how beneficial this quote unquote help was. The dark and mysterious Lord of mumbo-jumbo, Mathesus Loton, stepped up to the edge of the maze.

He reached out with one black leather gauntleted hand, and deftly caught the magic cloth creation in mid air. With his other hand, the vile wizard pulled the waistband of his baggy and flowing harem pants out from his body. He then stuffed the still tingling and straight-haired stuffy down his pants. For a brief (pun intended) moment, both Bartimon and Dibble Dobble felt sorry for the little cloth stuffy. But then Bartimon went to heal his mangled pinky, and thought the punishment befit the crime. Dibble Dobble's moment of pity faded as well, as he remembered his bruised cajones.

I hope the dark and mysterious pervert wets himself soon, thought the small servant. *Oh, the horrors! The horrors! Tee Hee Hee!* Dibble Dobble's wicked grin threatened to cause his face to crack. The distant sounds of three feathered fiends finally finding the final step of the tower stairway echoed up from below. Dibble Dobble started giggling madly at this point. All attempts at any form of composure were completely lost.

The waterfowl-version of bad language only made this worse, as the dastardly ducks quacked epithets of payback and revenge from ground level. By this time the vertically-challenged servant-to-wizards was howling with merriment, while tears flowed freely from his eyes and he thanked his stars that he wasn't wearing that two-faced mask right then..

Back in the maze, where the real action was taking place unobserved, Fred continued to drag Ralph along through the twists and turns of the large walled maze puzzle. By this time, the two rodents had searched all of the previously unvisited lanes of the maze except for the one they were currently on. And given the long hallways of this particular run, both mice were confident that the center of the maze was close.

"This might be it, Ralph," said Fred.

Still puffed out, and being dragged behind the star-decorated mouse, the darkened mouse responded, "Yes. And given my current condition, it looks like you are destined to win this challenge," said Ralph.

"That is not your fault, Ralph. Blame Mathesus. But I am perfectly willing to share my victory meal with you. Bartimon always conjures way too much mango and banana mix. There will be plenty to eat for both of us," said Fred.

"Wow!" said Ralph, suddenly sounding a whole lot happier. "That sounds really good right now. Thanks, Fred. You would not believe the crazy mess of slop that Mathesus tried to feed me the last time he summoned me."

"Was it bad?" asked Fred, as he continued to pull the blackened Ralph along a particularly long hallway in the maze.

"Bad?" exclaimed Ralph. "It would have gagged a maggot, and turned a cockroach to a vegan diet!"

"That sounds pretty awful there, Ralph. But do not worry. Bananas and mangoes are in your future. Look straight ahead," Fred said.

Ralph looked forward, and saw a wonderful sight. "Is that it?" asked Ralph.

"I think so. The center of the maze. The finish. And soon, the feasting place," said Fred.

The star-patterned mouse pulled the blackened puffball mouse to the end of the last hallway. As the first mouse crossed into the center of the maze the final magical effect of the Wizards of Old was triggered. Magic sky rockets appeared over the maze, erupting here and there. A veritable pyrotechnics display drew the attention of

The Worrisome War of the Whimsical Wizards   NM Reed & WL Preston

all parties back to the mouse maze.

Chapter TWELVE

Dibble Dobble looked on from the top of the tower. He was wiping the last of the tears of laughter from his eyes. Bartimon Montinair had just completed a magical healing spell on his mangled hand, when the fireworks went off. He looked to the maze's center to see who had won the race and was rather confused when he saw both mice together in the middle of the maze race course.

Mathesus Loton had been strapping down his brand-new wriggling bikini brief over his privates. The curvaceous orange-haired stuffy was beginning to realize that self-awareness for an animated cloth doll was not such a good thing. And there was indeed a form of hell for stuffies like itself.

Inside Mathesus Loton's pants had to be the first level. And the thought of being some form of absorbent pad for this perverted spell-slinger filled Zestful's cloth head with dread and terror. Perhaps that doddering old fool Bartimon would rescue him? Maybe not. Zestful had torqued the aged wizard's little finger really badly. Even Bartimon 'monkey brain' would not forgive and forget so soon.

Oooo- licck! Thought Zestful. *The pervert is leaking!* Zestful could feel herself getting damp all over. Oh, the horror!

And Mathesus thought, "Oh good! Just in time. My bladder was getting rather full. Now the doll can soak up my wetness issues. I wonder how much liquid the squirming magic item can hold before it leaks? I hope it doesn't vibrate like the one I have at home; that would be bad. But I shall have to refill my insides again. Then let go with the personal fire hose of mine. What a warm, friendly feeling I'm experiencing! No leaks so far! Wondrous! It is going to be a long day! "

Then Mathesus was surprised and startled by the

fireworks going off. So much so in fact, that his bowels decided to vacate any waste in that location. *Hmmm.* Thought Mathesus. *Too many prunes with breakfast. But, I now have a catch-pad for such accidental discharges. Yes! It is going to be a very long day!*

He looked up to see what was going on at the maze, while inside the pants of "Mr. Dark and Mysterious", Zestful was experiencing more disgusting sensations, and squirming fitfully in response. Indeed, this was hell for the cloth doll. The orange-haired creation was aware that the leather of its tiny shoes must be disintegrating at this point.

Oh, the horror!

Bartimon Montinair looked to the maze's center, where the two mice were. His mouse was at the very center, and the puffball mouse of Mathesus was off to one side, clutching the tail of his star-covered rodent. The goodly wizard reached out with his mind to reconnect with his summoned friend. He needed to know the actual outcome of the race. Had his mouse won? Bartimon would soon see.

Fred? thought Bartimon. *Did we perchance win this race?* Fred, suddenly tapped with Bartimon's mental presence in his little skull, thought, *I will tell you after the bananas and mangoes appear. You said if I won or lost, now, pay up, weird wizard!*

The goodly spell-caster made some interesting moves and gestures with both hands, and the center of the maze was suddenly filled with thick slices of fresh mango and bananas. Both mice immediately set to work doing what they did best. Eating. Even though Ralph's fur was still standing straight out from his body like a sea urchin, he was quite easily able to get at the veritable mountains of fruit all around him.

And Fred was tucking in as well.

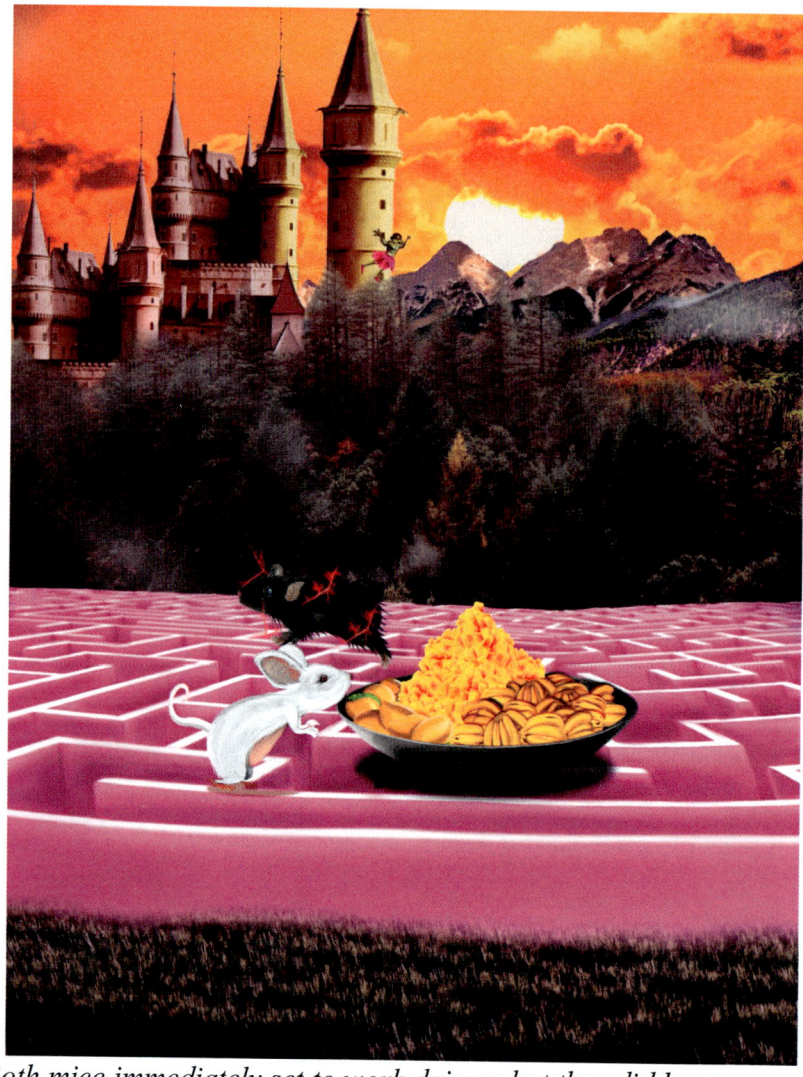

The Worrisome War of the Whimsical Wizards   NM Reed & WL Preston

"Both mice immediately set to work doing what they did best. Eating. Even though Ralph's fur was still standing straight out from his body like a sea urchin, he was quite easily able to get at the veritable mountains of fruit all around him. And Fred was tucking in as well."

The Worrisome War of the Whimsical Wizards

NM Reed & WL Preston

Chapter THIRTEEN

Yummy! Thought both mice.

We have found paradise! thought Ralph, his mouth full of half masticated banana.

Ummm... thought Bartimon. *Did we win, my furry friend?*

Fred thought back, *I am not sure. If this star-pattern on my fur were to go away suddenly, I am certain my recollection of the circumstances of this race's conclusion would become more clear.*

The mouse continued to feed contentedly, while Bartimon considered his options. *Let me try to understand this,* thought Bartimon. *OK, if I de-magic the impressive pattern of my own star-filled designs from your fur, you will tell me who won the race?*

Yes, thought Fred, still munching away.

And if I do not? thought Bartimon. *What then?*

Well, thought Fred. *I guess you will pay the ultimate price for a moment's inattention. You were supposed to be in a mental link with me throughout. You are supposed to be watching the race. And what was all that screaming about, just before the end of the race?"* inquired Fred, as he turned his attention to some banana.

One of my stuffies turned rebel, thought Bartimon. *My goodly friend Zestful did not agree with your giving assistance to the other mouse. He wanted me to stop you. I forgot to restrain him, and he mangled my right pinky finger, I am filled with sorrow over his rebellion. And I feel sorrow for his punishment, and* Bartimon shed some tears over the loss.

But Fred tried to be supportive. *You have no real control over that bratty doll, Bartimon,* thought Fred. "That orange-haired terror was made by one of your fore bearers. Either that megalomaniac, Metaphysical Matilda, or that wizardly whack-job Whimsy Williams, caused that miniature ruffian to come into existence.

Bartimon was momentarily dragged out of his remorse by questions filling his mind. *How do you know so much, my furry friend, Fred?*

Between bites of mango and banana, Fred thought back, *Many generations of my ancestors passed down many interesting details about you wizarding types. You summon us for your curious experiments. You give us silly tasks that no sane mouse would bother with. And often, we end up being victimized by your magically created servants. Did you know that Zestful enjoyed punting us mice around the hallways of your mountain hideout when no one was looking? That bratty punk was definitely cut from the wrong cloth. Speaking of which, where is that carrot-topped villain, anyway?"*

Bartimon glanced over in the direction of the tower, trying to form a mental picture of what Mathesus Loton was doing to Zestful at this moment. The goodly wizard stopped himself, knowing that some questions were best left unanswered.

He finally thought, *The orange-haired rebel is now in the hands of someone better equipped than I in dealing with his bad behavior. Someone who seems to be altogether worse than Zestful. Much worse.*

Bartimon gave an involuntary mental shudder at the thought of what must be going on over on the other side of the dueling field.

Fred stopped eating for a moment, contemplating the scattered thoughts of the wizard who had summoned him. A clear picture began to form in his rodent brain. *"You gave Zestful to that pervert? You turned over that cloth brute to an even bigger villain than himself? That carrot-topped pain-in-my-tail is now a plaything for Mathesus Loton?*

Yes, thought Bartimon sadly. *I am sorry to say he is.*

Fred was anything but sorry about this turn of events.

Woo-Hoo! thought the starry mouse. *There is indeed justice in the universe! Now that is a thunderbolt of karma-come-to-call ! Mice everywhere shall rejoice upon hearing the telling of this tale! Thank you, Bartimon! Your fashion sense may leave much to be desired, but your sense of what is right and wrong is unquestionable! Bravo, spell-caster! Bravo!*

And with that, Fred informed Ralph of the incredible news that the orange-haired terror was finally getting what it so richly deserved.

And suddenly, both Ralph and Fred were seized by a notion that threw millions of generations of rodent dignity on its ear. Both mice proceeded to do the rodent version of a happy-dance, though Ralph's dance steps were more like moon-walking. Bartimon was once more confused by the turn of events, but then he remembered his original thought.

Fred, thought Bartimon. *While I restore your fur to its original uninteresting color, could you answer me one question?*

Between dance steps that imitated the tango, Fred thought back, *Why yes, oh great and wise Bartimon Montinair, friend to mice everywhere. What is your question?*

Well, thought Bartimon, as he made magical gestures in the direction of Fred. *I was wondering. Who actually won the race?*

Fred glanced down at his fur as he spun himself to the right on his hind legs. As he continued with his outrageous display of ballroom antics, the mouse saw that the star pattern was fading from his fur. When it was completely gone, and his white fur and pink tail where the color they should be, Fred thought back to Bartimon, *I won,* thought Fred. *I dragged Ralph across the finish line, but I was the first to cross it. Now, if you don't mind, my good friend Ralph and I have a feast to enjoy. And thank you for the mangoes and bananas.* And with that, Fred did one more spin, then got back to what his kind did best. Eat.

"Well," said Bartimon aloud. "It seems I have won the first challenge of the duel."

Chapter FOURTEEN

Dibble Dobble, who had been too busy laughing to see the outcome of the race, decided to concede to the goodly wizard's observation. "I agree!" said Dibble Dobble into the metal speaking tube. "A clear victory indeed!"

Dibble Dobble turned his attention to Mathesus Loton, who seemed to be inspecting something in his black harem pants.

"Be there any questions as to the outcome of this first challenge?" said Dibble Dobble in his deepest official-sounding voice.

Mathesus looked up from his musings over the darkening condition of his squirming undergarment. Given the immobile condition he had left his summoned mouse in earlier, the dark wizard had expected an easy win by the Paisley Patron and his disco mouse.

"No," said Mathesus. "No question. Let us get on to the next challenge. My new sanitary napkin seems to be squirming with delight over its new duties of catch and absorb."

Dibble Dobble, Bartimon Montinair, both mice, and all three extremely bruised and ruffled ducks replied in chorus: "EWWW!!"

"That's it," said Ralph. "I'm done. Forget any appetite I might have had. I just want to leave. How about you, Fred?"

Fred was just finishing choking down his last bite of mango. "I think my overfull tummy may burst if I take one more bite. Let us depart this place of silliness, Ralph. Bartimon, if you would be so good as to return us to our homes, I would be ever so grateful. I must spread the word about your grand victory over the forces of evil and the sneaky orange-haired fiend. All of the surviving victims of the orange-haired terror will be celebrating its descent into hell.

"All right," said Bartimon. "I will send you home." Bartimon looked up to the tower. "If the other member of this wizards' duel has no objections?"

Dibble Dobble turned to look at Mathesus.

Mathesus replied, "No. No. Send the vermin where you will. I have no further use for mice." He looked down at his black trousers and patted something squirming at the crotch level. "I have other ideas in mind. Other possibilities of a cloth creation involving magic and angry bees. Oh, the sensations I shall experience! My stuffies shall be life-size!"

Mathesus stood proudly, with both fists on his hips, and his lower body thrust forward. The general reaction from all of the others present on the Blasted Plain was predictable.

"EWWWW!!" They all cried in unison.

Part 3
Chapter ONE

After the collective stomachs on the dueling Plain got done churning over the most recent immoral and sickening activity of Mathesus Loton, the vertically challenged servant- to-wizards announced the next challenge.

All considerations of stopping for a breakfast or lunch recess had fled from the mind of Dibble Dobble. He decided instead to keep the events of the dual moving. Maybe he would be hungry by afternoon.

Maybe.

Dibble Dobble raised the metal speaking cone to his mouth once again. In the deepest voice he could manage, he let all know the particulars of the next event.

"Round one has gone to the goodly wizard, Bartimon Montinair. And now, the two wizards shall pay heed to the words of the wizarding herald. That being me," he smiled.

"The next event shall involve the two combating spell casters summoning forth amphibians for a Frog Jumping Contest. Do both magic users understand the terms of the second round?"

There was a moment of silence from both wizards. Dibble Dobble looked first to Bartimon, and then to Mathesus. Neither said anything for a long time.

Finally, Mathesus broke the silence. "Say what?" he said. "First, a silly mouse maze race! Now, a frog jump?! What's next? Foursquare?! Hopscotch!? What kind of namby-pamby doofus duel is this? When do we get to the blood and guts of this thing? This is a dual between wizards! Not a playground dustup at an elementary school!"

Bartimon interjected, "I'll bet you were a bully at school! You villain! As for me, I would enjoy a good game of hopscotch!"

Mathesus was quick to respond. "And I'll bet your

underwear is pink and frilly, you wizardry wimp! I enjoyed stealing the toys and lunch money from losers like you in school! It made me the dark and mysterious Lord of Magic that I am today!"

Bartimon did not miss a beat. He said, "Lord of Madness, maybe. No doubt you were beaten so much by the teachers, that you started to enjoy it. That is what made you the sorry, misguided soul you are today!"

Mathesus retorted, "While you may be correct about the beatings, I have to inform you of a factor that has occurred to me concerning your origin. A conventional mother/father arrangement might have been your creation, but your child rearing was far from normal. More likely, you weren't born in the conventional manner at all. You are probably drop kicked out of the operating room, while the afterbirth was taken home and raised in place of you!"

Dibble Dobble jumped in before things got totally out of hand. Again.

"Gentlemen! This is not a contest of worrisome words and whimsical wills! This is a contest of wizardly might! Now, I shall call forth the next field of play, and you two spell casters shall summon forth your frogs. Now, I did state frogs, and I stated jumping. No poisonous toads! Do both parties understand?"

This last was directed at Mathesus Loton, for Dibble Dobble was certain that the dark and dastardly doofus was already trying to come up with some way to pervert the conditions of the contest.

And he was right..

Mathesus said, "Can I summon a Gila monster instead? They don't jump so much, but they are mostly my favorite color. Black, that is. Hmmm?"

"No!" said Dibble Dobble. "But you may alter your frog's coloring to suit your fancy, just as you did with your summoned mouse," said the short servant in his deepest voice.

"Oh," said Mathesus..

Bartimon perked up at this point. "So we are free to alter the color of our frogs as well? All righty then!"

A general groan was heard from Dibble Dobble, Mathesus, the ducks, and the magic bedpan. Dibble Dobble suddenly thought a little added advice might be needed. He raised the metal speaking tube to his mouth again and said, "Based on the last two summoning's by the dueling wizards, it might be advisable to keep the coloring of the summoned beings a little less, um, outrageous."

Both wizards answered at the same time.

"Outrageous?!"

Mathesus elaborated on this with a reactive response first. "I, Mathesus Loton, dark and mysterious weaver of that which is mystical and magical, have a very sound reason for my color choice !"

Dibble Dobble couldn't resist speaking to this. "And that is?" he said. "Do tell."

Mathesus, of course, had a quick answer. "Fashionable black goes with everything!" As if that was the universal answer to all questions of fashion.

Bartimon Montinair had other ideas when it came to the mystery of a wizard's wardrobe. "My festive choices are carefully calculated to inspire myself and others to endeavor to persevere in all that we do and say. The patterns and colors are chosen with happy thoughts in mind."

And, of course Mathesus had something to say in response. "Well, isn't that cute? I am so inspired with all my happy thoughts, I could just vomit."

Bartimon responded in kind. "On a field of so-called fashionable black, the residue of your color-filled expectoration would probably be a fashionable improvement.!"

Dibble Dobble jumped in once again. "Spell casters! I shall now call forth the field, upon which the tournament of the frog jump shall be played out! Please observe the dueling plain."

Chapter TWO

Dibble Dobble once again opened the box containing the magic wands. Following the instructions from the "voice from the cauldron", the short servant selected a wand marked "Leaping Field". Dibble Dobble took the wand over to the stone battlement of the tower roof and pointed it at the mouse maze. He said, "Frog Jump Field!"

A flash of light erupted from the end of the wand, and the large maze faded from existence. And before the eyes of Dibble Dobble and the two wizards, a series of grid-lines began to form on the Blasted Plain. After a few moments, numbers began to appear at regular intervals along the length of the leaping field. Dibble Dobble presumed that these numbers were for measurement purposes.

And he was right. Given the size of the grid, the servant-to-wizards had to wonder what other kinds of creatures had use this grid field. The 'voice of no one in particular' that issued forth from the wizards' cauldron had mentioned a few.

"The hobgoblin hop." "The Saurian Stomp". "The Minotaur muscle move." "The pixie pirouette."

And one that Dibble Dobble found particularly interesting, the "succubus slap and tickle". But, much to the short servant's dismay, the 'voice from the cauldron' refused to elaborate on the details of this last event. It left Dibble Dobble rather frustrated in some new ways.

Shaking the curvaceous images from his brain, Dibble Dobble raised the metals speaking cone to his mouth and spoke again. "The wizards will now call forth their frogs for the jumping contest!"

The wizards' servant looked to Bartimon first. True to form the paisley be-decked magic user with the good heart was putting many grand gestures into his spell making. Dibble Dobble was afraid Bartimon might hurt himself if the enchanter put any more effort into his conjuring. A moment after Bartimon finished with a ballet-like spin on his toes, a loud "proof" sound was heard by all on the Blasted Plain. A small puff of multi-hued smoke appeared at the starting line of the Leaping Field. Within seconds, the rainbow smoke cleared revealing Bartimon Montinair's summoned amphibian. Dibble Dobble, Mathesus Loton, the stuffies, the duck uglies, and even the magic bedpan were momentarily confused by the frog that Bartimon had summoned.

    Imagine a large frog from a lily pond. Then color the frog pink from bulge-eyed head to webbed foot. Then dress the poor creature in a small, pink paisley ballet tutu, with pink satin ballet slippers upon the hind feet. And as Dibble Dobble watched, the foot-long amphibian stood up on its hind legs and looked down at itself. It then croaked forth a short poem:

> "My name is Phil.
> Against my will,
> I am whammied here
> to sit and chill.
> My hue be pink.
> I am caused to think,
> that I've been coated
> with wizardly stink!"

    Dibble Dobble was just beginning to wonder if things could not get any more weird, when Mathesus Loton began his own version of magical conjuring. Sitting down upon the Blasted Plain, the black-clad wizard of mystery began playing upon his magic bedpan as though it were a set of bongo drums. The sound had a certain rhythm to it. But Dibble Dobble began to hear a noise like backing-up plumbing issuing forth from the magical item. There was a loud gurgling sound, and then the rushing noise of a large amount of liquid moving up from a long pipe. When the rhythmic beating of Mathesus Loton reached a musical peak, a black oil-like stream issued forth from the magic bedpan like a geyser. The fluid moved in a high arc through the air, landing next to the recently arrived frog named Phil.

Fortunately for the pink clad amphibian, he was able to jump out of the way before being splashed by the dark-colored liquid. When the last of the midnight hued stream was spent upon the starting line of the Leaping Field, Dibble Dobble noticed two things.

First, the fluid the Mathesus Loton had conjured from his curious magic device had the odor of a long fermenting cesspool. And he began gagging from the suddenly polluted air.

Secondly, the short servant could make out a small form moving at the center of the splash zone. At first, it seemed to struggle ineffectively upon the ground. Within a few moments, a small frog-shaped form could be seen by all on the playing field. It rose to a standing position on its hind legs, and began using its front legs to clear off the stinking goo from its body. When it had removed enough of the sewage from itself so that it might see and speak, the object of Mathesus Loton's spell-working spewed forth its own verbal foulness for all to hear::

"Mathesus!" It yelled. "Do you have to use the "Magic Plumber" spell? I am not a turd in the punch bowl, you idiot!"

The sewage darkened frog continued to wipe, as best he could, at its offal-coated body. Bartimon, Phil the frog, Dibble Dobble, and the duck uglies were all doing their best not to breathe in the recently polluted air. Mathesus seemed to be sniffing it thoughtfully, as one might do when trying to decide which perfume to wear. The stuffies and the magic bedpan were thankful that breathing was one thing

The Worrisome War of the Whimsical Wizards   NM Reed & WL Preston

they were spared from doing.

Chapter THREE

Bartimon finally came to the rescue of all of the air breathers on the Blasted Plain. From his "CROW ROYA" bag of purple, the paisley bedecked wizard pulled out a multicolored parasol. Bartimon opened it quickly, exposing a canopy that was colored like a rainbow.

As Dibble Dobble watched, Bartimon began to spin his magic umbrella while intoning some mystical words. He faced the top of the bumbershute at the smelly frog, spinning it like a large fan. A perfume-filled breeze began to blow across the Blasted Plain, from Bartimon to the sewage coated amphibian..

Almost at once, Dibble Dobble could sense a great change in the quality of the local air. The reek of flush-able spew was rapidly being replaced by the smell of a large bouquet of roses. All on the field of wizardly battle were thankful, with one noteworthy exception..

The magic user clad in black was having a different reaction altogether. He began sneezing violently. Between the great blasts from his nose and mouth, Mathesus Loton managed to utter a few words.

"Roses!"
(sneeze!)
"Not Roses!"
(Sneeze twice!)
"Bartimon!"
(Sneeze thrice!)
"Stop!"
(Sneeze four times with lots of boogers flying!)

Bartimon Montinair was seen to think about this turn of events for a few moments, while a sly smile began to play across his face. He then thought the better of it, stopping the spin of his parasol and putting it back in his magic purple bag.

Mathesus Loton collapsed any heap, while gasping for breath. Dibble Dobble noted the foul scents of earlier were gone, and the intense smell of roses was beginning to fade as well. He lifted the metal speaking tube to his mouth and addressed Bartimon Montinair.

"Goodly wizard! Thank you for clearing the air. Your actions are most appreciated." Dibble Dobble could hear the duck uglies quacking their agreement with this from the base of the tower.

He silently wondered if they would be bird- brained enough to try a second assault on his place of refuge at the top. Then he thought, that, considering their currently magically altered forms, they just might and he quickly stepped over and secured the trap door against any further interruptions by any angry avians.

The small servant then turned to the black-clad heap of wizardly clothing on the ground. He raised the metal speaking cone to his mouth again, this time addressing Mathesus Loton.

"Oh, dark and mysterious maker of magic! It seems that one of your dark secrets has lost its mystery. You are dreadfully allergic to roses. How interesting. I must ask before we continue. Are you able to go on? Or shall we cancel the race and declare the winner?"

A wicked smirk was dancing on the hooded face of Dibble Dobble, while he hopped a few happy steps on his stilts.

As he watched, the black-clad wizard began to raise himself to a seated position. After shaking his head back and forth a few times, in an obvious attempt to clear it, Mathesus finally spoke.

"Bartimon! You dimwit! How dare you attack me in such a manner! I sneezed so hard, I have fouled my curvaceous redheaded and zestful codpiece beyond all possibility of repair! *And* it has stopped its struggling! I may have pooped and peed it to death, and what a waste for such a well-made vibrating undergarment"!

Without preamble, the others on the Blasted Plain observed a moment of thoughtful silence for the recently departed stuffy.

Bartimon thought, "Oh, Zestful! I shall miss you."

The duck uglies thought, "Ooooo! Ick!"

The magic bedpan thought, "At least you have the option of dying after such treatment. You do not want to know the kinds of foul stuff he has put in me!"

The group of stuffies near Bartimon stood silently and lowered their heads. The collective thoughts did not actually reflect their somber mood. *Better you than us, you orange haired Prima Donna.*

Dibble Dobble too had lowered his head, but with not a trace of regret upon his face. "Call that karmic payback, you magic nutcracker. Mathesus did me the greatest favor ever! Hoorah!"

Chapter FOUR

The short servant recovered from his joyful reverie and returned to the matter at hand. He raised the metal speaking tube to his mouth, and said, "Goodly wizard's! Let us tarry not a moment longer! Let us all focus our attentions on the two frogs on the Leaping Field. Now! Are you two amphibians prepared to begin?"

Phil raised a frog equivalent of a thumb in the air to signify that he was ready. The darkly stained frog raised the frog equivalent of the middle finger in reply. Considering what this poor frog had already been subjected to just getting here, Dibble Dobble decided to let that one go without comment.

He spoke into the metal cone once again. "The frogs will now take their places at the starting line. A series of three jumps will be preformed by each summoned competitor. The most distance covered by either of the frogs shall signify a winner to this challenge. Now! On your marks!"

The frog in the ballet costume named Phil obediently took his place at the starting line. Dibble Dobble noted that the amphibian was having some difficulty walking in his ballet slippers. The darkened, and as yet unnamed, frog grudgingly took his place next to his competitor.

Unheard by the wizards, Dibble Dobble, the duck uglies, the stuffies, and even the magic bedpan, Phil whispered to his fellow frog. "Sid. You are definitely going to win this one. That harebrained Bartimon has magic ballet shoes on my webbed feet. And they are killing me! I can hardly walk let alone ump! Good luck, my friend."

Sid whispered back, "Stuff your luck, you embarrassment to the Lily pad! I am going to lose this on purpose. You winning this race, dressed as you are, will be the ultimate payback for that Pervert in Black! Now," as he lowered himself down for his first leap, "let's make this look good!"

As he took note that the frogs looked to be ready, Dibble Dobble said, "GO!" Into the speaking tube. Both frogs launched themselves into the air, flying over the measured markings as they went. Sid had thrown himself a goodly distance down the field. Phil, hampered as he was in tightly fitting pink footwear, could not match his fellow frog in measure.

In fact, Dibble Dobble noted, the pink frog barely covered half the distance. It looked to the small servant that "Mr. Dark and Dastardly" might win this race.

That did not sit well with Dibble Dobble. He first looked to Bartimon for his reaction to the first round. The paisley- bedecked wizard looked worried. Dibble Dobble then looked to Mathesus Loton to assess his reaction. The black clad wizard was rubbing his black gloved hands together appreciatively.

Dibble Dobble gulped down his growing fear, and raised the metal cone to his mouth again. "Round two! Frogs, take your marks! Ready?"

Once again, as the two amphibians took their places at the starting line, Phil raised a thumb. Sid blew a raspberry with his very long tongue. Dibble Dobble decided to let the second transgression to decorum go as well. The poor frog was obviously feeling pretty crappy as well as smelly that way.

Sid again whispered so that only Phil could hear, "all right. I've got your leap pinned. Now. Leap like you just did, and I will cut my leap by half. It will be a tie. Ready?"

Phil, wincing in pain as he whispered back, replied, "I'll do what I can. I think my feet have fallen asleep."

Dibble Dobble spoke again into the metal cone, saying, "GO!"

This time, Sid held back, letting Phil go first. The pink

The Worrisome War of the Whimsical Wizards   NM Reed & WL Preston

frog did his best, but could only cover half the distance he had covered before. Sid, gulping down his own personal pride, flopped himself into the air in a halfhearted attempt to half his opponents jump. He managed, but just barely.

At the same time, a complaint was heard coming from the direction of the wizard in black. "Sid!" He said. "You call that a leap? My three legged dog Lucky could jump twice that distance! Put more effort in, or I will be having frog legs in garlic butter for dinner!"

Bartimon, noting that his frog Phil had won the second round, was much more appreciative in his remarks. "Philip! Well done! I shall cast a spell of fly attraction at your victory party! You shall feast well dear friend!"

Phil, limping slowly back to the starting line, whispered. "Sid, I will gladly share my flies with you. Thank you for throwing this race."

Sid, whispering in response, said, "Stick your flies in your frog butt, pink skin. I am not doing this for you. Besides, you ever get a whiff of Mr. dark and dull-witted over there? The stink on him always brings a cloud of flies waiting in the wings. Or better, on the wings, if you get my meaning. Now. Third time's a charm. Let's do this!"

When Dibble Dobble saw that the two pond dwellers had taken their marks, he raised the speaking device again, saying, "GO!" For the third and final time.

Sid timed his shortened leap to coincide with Phil's, but had no way of predicting what was about to happen to his fellow competitor.

As Phil made his final move to leap, hoping to claim victory, Fate had other ideas. Both of Phil's tightly tied ballet shoes gave up the ghost at the same instant. The thin pink straps snapped, causing the pink frog to lose all traction in his hind legs. His leap was more of a flop, as he only managed to move forward one fro- body length of distance.

Sid, unable to stop his airborne arc, landed six times

the distance down the leaping field. He had tried to lose, and had instead given victory to the wizardly pervert, Mathesus.

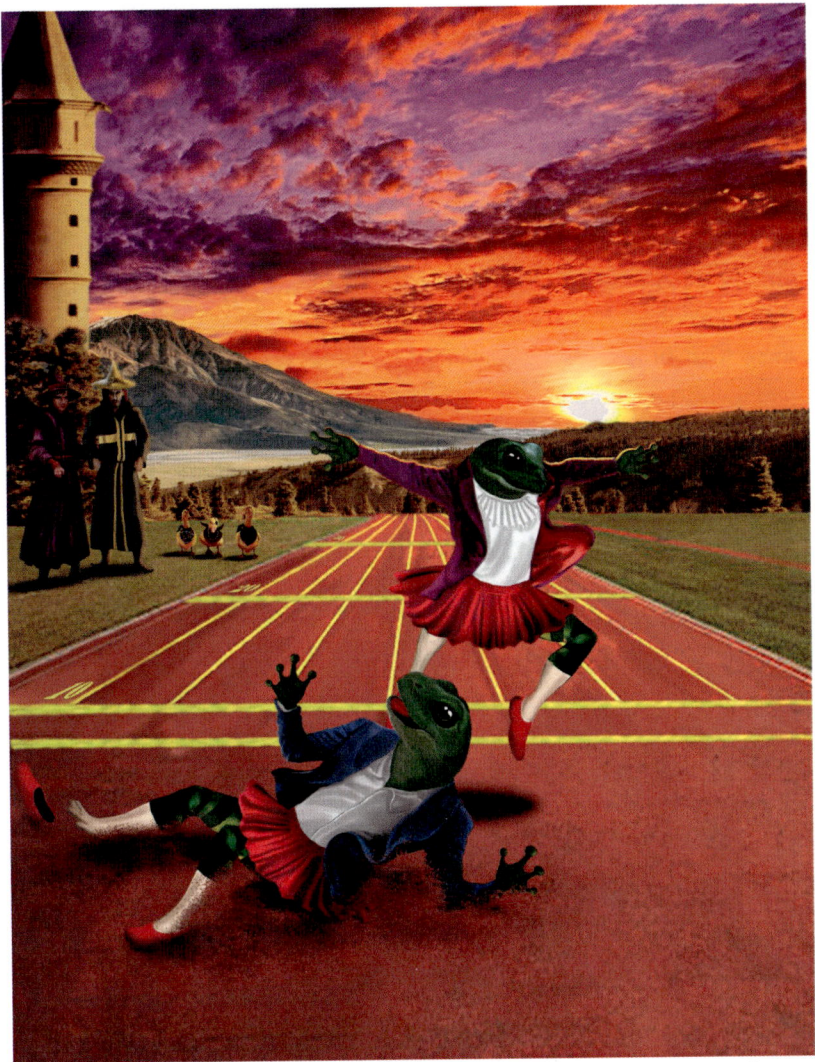

The Worrisome War of the Whimsical Wizards — NM Reed & WL Preston

"The thin pink straps snapped, causing the pink frog to lose all traction in his hind legs. His leap was more of a flop, as he only managed to move forward one fro- body length of distance."

Dibble Dobble slowly raised the speaking cone to his mouth, in order to utter words he had to fight with himself to say.

"The winner of the second challenge is Mathesus Loton. The contest is, thus far, all even at one win to one win. The next event shall be the deciding challenge. The winner shall claim all of the losers possessions. The loser shall move to the far side of the Planet, and live out his days in exile."

Chapter FIVE

Dibble Dobble cast about for an idea. A quick plan that just might fit with his scheme of *having it all*. Then he glanced at the goodly wizard, Bartimon Montinair. The paisley bedecked magic user was downcast. His head was tilted forward, with his lower lip sticking out in a pout. The vertically challenged servant couldn't bring himself to rob him blind.

But Mathesus, on the other hand, was another matter.

Dibble Dobble glanced over at the spell-caster in black and the perverted magician was dancing around, in celebration of his victory in the frog jump. Mathesus had peeled off the soiled and expired stuffy named zestful, and was swinging the heavily polluted item over his head. The magic bedpan was issuing forth some kind of stripper style burlesque music to punctuate the dance of the man in black. Mathesus was just about to remove more clothing, thus damaging the sanity of the short servant even more, when an idea struck Dibble Dobble like a thunderbolt.

Before he could speak though, both wizards stopped what they were doing and addressed the wizarding Herald on the teetering tower.

Mathesus was first, naturally. "Wait a second there!" He said, as he gave the destroyed stuffy a final swing over his head and released it like a sling stone. Dibble Dobble watched as the brown and yellow stained stuffy corpse flew toward the tower through space. He was rewarded with the sound of the duck uglies squawking and quacking loudly. Obviously, Mathesus had scored a direct hit on the fowl villains. There were several moments thereafter of unhappy duck noises.

Dibble Dobble smirked in response, while looking to Mathesus in reaction to his inquiry. Mathesus went on, "I thought you said this was a six event challenge? Now it is only three? Why?"

Bartimon Montinair echoed Mathesus' sentiments in this latest development. "Yes!" He said. "Why? I was looking forward to more interesting contests of wizardry. Please do not rob us of the fun of competitive spell-casting."

That last comment got an immediate reply from Mathesus. "Competitive spell-casting? You paisley painted poopoo head! This is a dual! A *dual*! We are not here for fun! We are in this desolate place to bring an end to one or the other of us! Speaking of which," he turned his attention back to Dibble Dobble, "are we now, finally, going to get to the blood and guts of this farce? Can we both step out from our opposite sides of this silly tower, and blast each other with fire and bolts of lightning? HUH? Can we?! Huh can we?!"

The sickening glee in Mathesus Loton's voice, with this last statement, made Dibble Dobble's stomach do a slow roll to the left side of his small body.

Oh well, thought the short servant on stilts, *so much for any ideas about lunch.*

Dibble Dobble raised the speaking device to his mouth. He said, "The Herald of Wizardry, that being me, has arrived at a judgment. Given the interesting shows of spell-casting thus far by both combatants, it is the decision of the Herald to call upon both parties in this dual to have one, and only one, more challenge between you. The wizards shall keep their respective places on either side of the Tower of Observance. From their places on the Blasted Plain, the wizards shall perform their greatest and most strenuous feats of magical summoning now. They shall each call forth a dragon of immense size."

Looking first at Bartimon, and then to Mathesus, Dibble Dobble finished his speech with, "What say you to this?"

Bartimon looked confused for a moment, but finally replied with, "Well. All righty then. If that is the way it has to be, so be it."

Mathesus was much more enthusiastic with his reply. The wizard in black jumped up and down, saying, "Yes! Yes! Stomp! Claw! Bite! Blast! Yes! Yes! Yes! Whoop! Whoop!"

Dibble Dobble bowed his hooded head in reply to each of the magician's responses. A small smirk played across the face of the short servant. He could not wait until the final part of his devious moment of genius to come into play.

But first, he thought to himself, *the summoning of the dragons.*

Chapter SIX

Speaking into the metal cone again, Dibble Dobble said, "The dueling wizards shall now call forth their dragons. The larger, the better. Now, begin!"

He then watched as both wizards went into their respective acts. Bartimon's casting took the form of foursquare game being drawn in the ash coated Plain before him. He then commanded his small army of stuffies to divide themselves equally into the foursquare's. Bartimon then began to draw forth his magical instruments from his "CROW ROYA" bag of purple velvet. He distributed the magical items equally amongst the stuffies, keeping a golden trumpet for himself at the last.

He said to the stuffies, loud enough for Dibble Dobble to hear, the following words, "Since our dear departed friend Zestful is no longer with us to play his part in the conjuring band, I, myself, shall have to play the lead trumpeteer."

Dibble Dobble could see, by way of nods and other telling body language, that the Army of stuffies seemed to be happy about the arrangement.

Perhaps, thought Dibble Dobble, *that little redheaded putz wasn't well-liked by the other stuffies either. Goody goody good! A good end to bad rubbish!*

The small servant looked on as Bartimon and his all-stuffy band began to play. And oh what a sound they made! To refer to the noise that issued forth from that side of the Blasted Plain as music would have been insulting to all real musicians everywhere, long dead, recently dead, living, or yet to be born. And Dibble Dobble plugged his ears as best he could, but shrill notes continued to rattle the molars in his mouth.

The small servant looked over to the wizard in black to see what he was about. Dibble Dobble could just barely make out what Mathesus Loton was saying in response to the horrendous cacophony that was issuing forth from the far side of the Blasted Plain.

Mathesus said, "That has to be the best imitation of the sound one makes when committing an unnatural act on a small animal in the woods on a moonless night. I rather like it! I wonder if they know the Symphony of the angry bee?"

As Dibble Dobble watched, the wizard of dark and mysterious perversions set about preparing his own grand casting. Rummaging through the folds in his dark colored robes, Mathesus began bringing forth all manner of curious and bizarre items. An 8 foot bullwhip with the words "beat me, baby" stenciled on the handle. An 8 foot ostrich plume with the words "tickle me, baby" on its handle. An 8 foot long, 4 foot wide booklet of paper with the words, "make me write bad checks, baby" on the cover.

Dibble Dobble's brain was reeling at the size and weirdness of each item not knowing the purpose of any of them as Mathesus continued to bring out his props for conjuring. The last, and most bizarre yet, was an 8 foot brass horn, with the words, "blow me, baby" printed on the side.

The dark and dastardly magician then hooked one end of an 8 foot rubber hose to the mouthpiece of the horn. Dibble Dobble could just make out the words printed on the side of this hose, "stuff this where the sun don't shine, baby" was the mysterious legend on this length of rubber tubing.

Without further ado, Mathesus stuffed the other end of the rubber hose, indeed, "where the sun don't shine, baby". From its position behind the wizard, the short servant could only presume that the rubber hose was occupying a place between the cheeks of the spell users backside.

"Well," thought Dibble Dobble, "everyone has his own

way of "tooting their horn." "

As the wizard in black began to coil and lick an 8 foot string of pearls, the short servant on stilts decided that ignorance was bliss, and then he averted his gaze from the spectacle of grand perverted magic. Dibble Dobble was certain his sanity would thank him later for this action.

As the noise from Bartimon and his magical band seemed to be reaching its musical finale, even more disturbing sounds began issuing forth from Mathesus' side of the Blasted Plain.

Dibble Dobble decided to clean up the previous events playing field. Reaching once more into the wooden box full of wands, the vertically challenged servant selected a wand marked "clean slate", then walked over to the edge of the tower roof. Without clearly surveying the Leaping Field to make certain it was clear of all beings, summoned or otherwise, Dibble Dobble spoke the words, "clean slate".

He quickly had a moment of regret. But only a moment. He recalled that the "voice of no one in particular" that issued forth from the wizards cauldron had advised him to make certain that any changes to the playing fields of the Blasted Plain be made when all summoned participants had been sent back to their origins by the wizards, and that any non-summoned beings that were on the field risked great bodily harm if they were "in the wax" when any wand-created changes were made.

Well, as was stated, Dibble Dobble had a moment of regret.

But only just a moment. As the wand did its thing, the Leaping Field began to fade. Dibble Dobble could see that the two summoned frogs had been magicked back to their homes by the wizards. But, for whatever reason, the three duck uglies had decided to waddle out onto the field.

As the Leaping Field continued to fade, the three dastardly ducks bandits began to thrash about and quack frantically.

Their cries could not be heard over the horrendous sounds currently being produced by both wizards. The small servant watched as the field continued to fade away, and the ducks thrashed about more wildly. When the 'Field of Leaping' had finally faded from existence, leaving behind the Blasted Plain of ash, Dibble Dobble could just make out three duck shaped forms buried in the ashes.

"Well," thought the servant, "not completely buried." All three of the thieves- transformed- into- ducks had been mostly covered as they had passed on to whatever existence there is after leading such fowl lives. Three upright duck bills and three sets of upright webbed feet protruded from the surface of the Blasted Plain. Dibble Dobble glanced at the 'clean slate' wand in his hand, wondering again at the irony of the universe.

He then put the wand back in with the others in the wood box, and closed the lid. Briefly, Dibble Dobble contemplated stealing the whole box. But then he glanced at the three 'Peeking' ducks.

Common sense and a profound sense of self preservation made him cast aside any possible ideas of theft.

"Besides," thought Dibble Dobble, "I still might end up with a whole load of loot if my nefarious scheme works out. It all depends on the dragons."

A thoughtful moment hit the short servant right between the eyes.

"Yes," he thought. "The dragons. The big, scaly, clawed, fanged, fire-breathing, bad attitude dragons. Oh boy....."

Things got suddenly quite depressing for Dibble Dobble. But before he could even think of a better, less dangerous plan, the summoning spells of both wizards went off with a big flash of sparks, a loud ear damaging bang, resulting in a soft whimper of dread from Dibble Dobble.

And there on the Blasted Plain appeared two huge towering forms of scaled nastiness that blotted out the sun from the small servant's point of view from atop the tower.

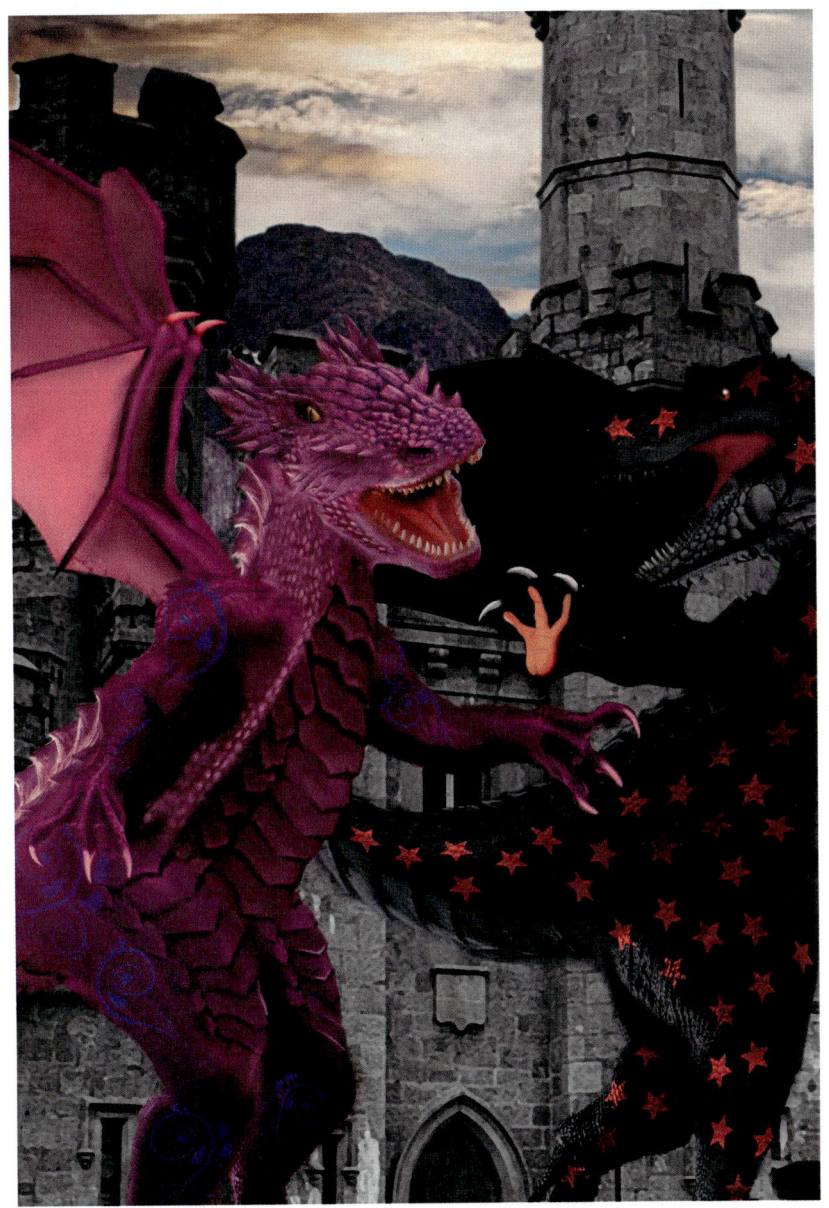

The Worrisome War of the Whimsical Wizards   NM Reed & WL Preston

" And there on the Blasted Plain appeared two huge towering forms of scaled nastiness that blotted out the sun from the small servant's point of view from atop the tower. "

The Worrisome War of the Whimsical Wizards					NM Reed & WL Preston

Chapter SEVEN

Easily equal to the height of the Tower of Observance, the two dragons began looking about themselves, surprise clearly showing in their large sparkling eyes.

The one Dragon, black as a piece of midnight, had obviously been summoned by Mathesus.

The other, was, well, pink from head to foot.

Oh crap, thought Dibble Dobble. *Bartimon has done it again. That addled-brained doofus may manage to get himself killed yet.*

The small servant shook his head in bewilderment, as he watched the two dragons finally turn and look at each other.

"Blackivar!" Boomed the pink Dragon. "Good to see you again! How is the family?"

The Black Dragon was blinking as he looked at the pink Dragon. He then shook his head to clear it, for it was obvious that his mind could not believe what his eyes were showing it.

"Rakival? Is that you? Are you sick or something?" The Black Dragon took an involuntary step backward, nearly squashing Mathesus Loton under his tail.

The black clad wizard rolled out of the way just in time, ending up in a seated position spitting up dust and ash.

The Black Dragon, not noticing the wizard at all, continued to address his pink counterpart. "Uhm,.. It's not catching, is it?"

The pink Dragon looked confused for a moment, then addressed the Black Dragon as though nothing was out of the ordinary. "Is what catching? I feel fine. Explain yourself, Blackivar."

"Well," said the Black Dragon, "either you are in need of a massive scale-darkening salon session, or some dimwitted wizard has altered your color to match his own idiotic idea of fashion sense."

The pink Dragon looked down at itself and grunted with obvious disgust. "That hare-brained Bartimon must have done this. But at least he didn't paint me with a paisley pattern."

Bartimon looked up with wonderment in his eyes. "A paisley Dragon!?" He said aloud. "What a wonnnderful idea!" The wizard quickly waved both hands in a dramatic fashion over his head. And a loud "pop" was heard.

"There!" He announced.

The Black Dragon and Mathesus Loton began to snicker loudly. The now paisley pink Dragon spoke, saying, "Oh no. I am not even going to look."

Addressing the Black Dragon, he said, "Oh, shut up Blackivar! This is not funny!"

And this only served to cause the Black Dragon to laugh uncontrollably. Holding his sides, great roars of hilarity peal forth from his ivory filled mouth. Mathesus Loton is also laughing out loud, though keeping a wary eye on the tail of the Black Dragon.

The new color-altered Dragon says, "This is totally embarrassing!" He looked about the Blasted Plain. His gaze finally coming to rest on the form of Bartimon Montinair.

"As I thought! Bartimon! You Dingle doodle! Would you care to explain why you have chosen to make me the laughing stock of all Dragon kind? And why have you summoned me in the first place?" He glanced over at the Black Dragon and the black-clad wizard.

"And you too can shut the hell up any time now!"

This pronouncement only served to cause both the Black Dragon and his wizard-summoner to fall on the ground, laughing even louder. The paisley- painted Dragon then leveled his gaze at Bartimon once again.

"Well?"

Bartimon Montinair does his best to stand firm as he addresses the Dragon, but it is obvious that he is a bit nervous at the moment.

The stuffy band of players take their immediate leave from the field of danger by diving en masse into the purple "CROW ROYA" bag, and Bartimon's lip begins to quiver as he notices that he is standing alone in front of an obviously pissed off Dragon. Summoning up what little courage he has, the paisley-bedecked wizard does his best to answer the questions put to him.

"I have summoned you here so you may take part in the final round of a dueling contest. You are to test your strength and dexterity against the other Dragon. The winners shall determine the overall victor of the contest. We have had two events thus far. I won the first, and Mathesus Loton has won the second. A tie stands between us at this point. Is that enough of an explanation, Goodley and mighty Rakival?"

The upset Dragon towering over Bartimon thought on this for a moment, then replied, "Your fear-filled babble only answers half of my questions. I am known to all as Rakival the Red, not Rakival the Paisley. Be so good as to be returning me to my factory original color, wizard Bartimon. You might recall from our last summoning session that I did not, and do not, enjoy having anything about me changed. Especially by some half-baked spell-slinger like you, Bartimon!"

The wizard plucked up whatever courage he could and replied with, "But it is only for the duration of the contest. And paisley is so festive."

The Dragon slowly tapped a paw in annoyance. Dibble Dobble could feel the vibration as it shook the teetering tower. He grabbed onto a battlement at the edge of the roof. It was a vain attempt at a secure position, and he knew it.

The paisley-bedecked Dragon finally spoke, after a few thoughtful moments of tapping. "Festive?" the Dragon said. "Festive? All right Bartimon. Here is the deal. You summoned me here, so I have to do your bidding. But your summoning spell will run out of magic power in a while, and I will be free to do as I please. And it will please me greatly to do a festive war dance on your spine, reducing you to a paisley patterned patch of pasture."

The Dragon leaned forward until he was nose to, well, body of the wizard. "Now decide! Return me to my beautiful shade of blood red, or suffer me later as a dance partner! And I will lead, Bartimon! Oh! How I will lead! And all of my dance steps will be on *you*! So think quickly, you paisley pile of poop!"

Bartimon, obviously even more unnerved by this latest turn of events, gives in quickly by saying, "Oh, very well. I just wanted to get into the spirit of it all!"

Rakival, still eye to eye with Bartimon said, "one more moment in this bizarre color pattern, and I can promise you that you will get all the way into the spirit of it. The Spirit World to be exact! Now do your silly wizard stuff and un-whammy my hide!"

Bartimon said, as he waved his hands over his head dramatically, "As you wish, oh, Crimson Terror."

A loud magical 'pop' is heard. Rakival, now once again the Red, examines himself and hums with approval.

"Crimson Terror? Hmmm... I like that! I will have to use that from now on! Now! What is the challenge?"

Chapter EIGHT

Mathesus and Blackivar, having recovered their composure somewhat, return themselves to standing positions. Mathesus, still wiping the tears of laughter from his eyes, says, "Yes! The challenge! What shall it be?" He then looked to the Tower of Observance for a reply.

But before Dibble Dobble could answer, Blackivar the Dragon had a few words of his own in response. "I am so glad he asked that question."

Pointing a six foot long black claw at Mathesus, Blackivar stated, "If it were up to Mr. Dark and Mysterious here, I have no doubt that oiled pigs and shaved baboons would be involved."

Mathesus attempted to speak in his own defense by saying, "Now wait just a moment!"

But the two dragons carried on their own dialogue, ignoring the black-clad wizard completely.

Rakival said, "Don't tell me he tried something weird with you?"

Blackivar's replied, "All right. I won't tell you. But it was weird. Very weird."

Rakival asked, "What happened?"

"I reminded Mathesus," said Blackivar, "about the summoning spell time limit, just like you did with Bartimon."

"Yeah?" said Rakival. "And what did you threaten the little pervert with?"

Blackivar said, "That I would turn his mountain hideaway into a crematorium."

"Wow!" said Rakival. "So he let you go?"

"Yes," said Blackivar. "It seems a little deviant did not want to make a total ash of himself."

Both huge dragons burst out laughing, shaking the entire Blasted Plain.

"Whoop! Whoop!" Chortled Rakival. "I love it!"

Dibble Dobble chose this moment to make his presence known. "Uhmm... You're two greatnesses? If I might say something please?"

The two dragons turned and said "What?" in stereo, then turned to look at the small person on the teetering tower.

"Well," said Dibble Dobble. "I need to inform the two titanic tragedies that walk the details of the challenge."

Rakival looks over at Blackivar and says, "You hear that Blackivar? Now we are two titanic tragedies that walk. These colorful titles just keep rolling in."

The red Dragon then looked back at the small servant on stilts and said, "And the details? Let me guess. A battle. Right? All teeth and claws and breath weapons? Well, until we have an agreement, in writing, that the wizards will do their magic mumbo-jumbo to restore the loser of the battle to health and well-being afterward, there will be no battle. Are we agreed on that?"

There was a moment of silence as Dibble Dobble let the dragon's words soak in. Fortunately, his plan called for something much less drastic than claws and fire-breathing. He said, "Ac---tually, the challenge will be much more simple than that. The two dragons shall test their strength and dexterity in....." Dibble Dobble paused for dramatic effect.

Blackivar said, "In what? I hate dramatic pauses, they make me want to spit acid at villages! Out with it, shrimp! What?!"

Dibble Dobble, his right stilt threatening to fail beneath him out of sheer terror, said, "A thumb fight!"

There was a long silence as the words made their way through the collective consciousnesses on the Blasted Plain. Then, all at once, the dragons, the wizards, and even the magic bedpan said, "WHAT?!"

Chapter NINE

Dibble Dobble said into the speaking cone, "You heard me correctly. A thumb fight." He looked first to the Red Dragon, and then to the Black Dragon, saying, "Between you two mighty and noble beings."

Rakival turned to Blackivar and said, "You hear that Blackivar? Now we are mighty and noble. This just keeps getting better and better." He then looked back at Dibble Dobble, saying, "And what does the winner get? The winning wizard and his Dragon, that is."

Dibble Dobble said, "Well, uhm, this dual is between the two wizards. Any sharing of the winnings will have to be discussed between the magic user and his dragon. Its not for me to decide."

Blackivar rubbed his belly for affect, saying, "I am getting a serious case of acid reflux here. Unless you want you and that tower to be a puddle of sizzling goo, I suggest you tell us what the winner gets."

Dibble Dobble answered quickly. "All of the loser's property. Magical, material, and monetary. You know, gold and stuff?"

Blackivar retorted with an edge, actually several edges, to his voice. "Yeah, shrimp. Most dragons know what *monetary* means. And when it comes to gold, there has been a long-standing misunderstanding amongst you little people. We actually prefer gemstones. Diamonds, especially."

Dibble Dobble was confused. "Diamonds are a dragons best friend?"

Both Blackivar and Rakival said, "Don't go there!"

Rakival then said, "And the loser? What does the losing wizard get?"

Dibble Dobble confidently replied, "The loser must go to the other side of the Planet for the rest of his days."

Both dragons let this sink in, as they turned and looked at Bartimon and then at Mathesus. Then they looked at each other and nodded. A knowing smile was on both of their scaled faces.

Rakival, after winking at Blackivar, and receiving a wink in return, said to Dibble Dobble, "So if Bartimon Montinair wins, he gets all of Mathesus Loton's loot? And Mathesus will be banished from this land forever?"

Rakival again looks at Blackivar. Knowing nods and smiles are exchanged.

Dibble Dobble, watching the silent exchange between the two dragons, nods knowingly to each of them, saying, "Yes. It all depends on who wins this challenge now. As Bartimon mentioned this duel was thus far tied at one win to one win. This shall be the deciding event."

Rakival gives a knowing wink to the small servant, then said, while looking at the Black Dragon, "Well now! Blackivar the Bold is a very strong and dexterous Dragon! I may not be enough of a match for him!"

Blackivar, blatantly showing off, rears back on his hind legs. He then began performing a number of muscle poses that would terrify any weightlifter. Dibble Dobble, the wizards, and even the bedpan, could all hear the sound of flesh and scales popping and rippling.

Dibble Dobble's and Bartimon's knees started knocking. Mathesus Loton was becoming noticeably aroused. The magic bedpan could not be reached for comment.

Mathesus while staring at Blackivar and drooling, was heard to say, "So does that mean you are giving up, Red Tide? Are you throwing in the towel?"

Rakival turned to Mathesus and said, "Giving up? *Me*? Never! For the honor of Bartimon Montinair shall I fight to the last! As for towels, you should use one, you slobbering pervert!"

The Worrisome War of the Whimsical Wizards   NM Reed & WL Preston

Chapter TEN

Dibble Dobble brought the speaking cone to his mouth and said, "All right then. Will the two combatants please take your positions for the Thumb Fight Royale!"

Blackivar and Rakival both say, "Yes!", And then proceed to make a big show of the fight to come. They circle each other. They snort. They growl. They kick rotting duck yuck at one another. All the while they are performing this act for the two dimwitted wizards, Dibble Dobble does his best not to laugh out loud, because he knows the secret.

Finally, after several moments of wrestler's silliness, the two dragons stop and face each other near the Tower of Observance. Tipping back on their hind legs, they raise their upper torsos high over the tower's battlements at its top.

Then Rakival and Blackivar extend one arm-like upper limb towards one another, and lock their paws in imitation of the classic thumb fight pose.

From their vantage points on the ground, neither wizard could see something interesting about the dragons. A noteworthy absence of physicality was in evidence here. And as Dibble Dobble could clearly see from the top of the tower, this whole contest would be a grand sham.

For the dragons had no thumbs!

When the two dragons looked to the short servant for the signal to go, he simply waved one hand downward in reply. The other hand was firmly placed over his mouth, in an attempt to stop any laughter from escaping.

The two dragons began pushing and pulling at one another. This goes on in an even manner for several minutes, then they really start making it look like no one or the other of them is losing the battle. This play acting nearly gets to the stage of utter ridiculousness.

Rakival cries aloud, "Ha! The tide is turning Blackivar! I have you now! One more moment and you shall cry for mercy! Admit it to yourself! You have lost!"

Blackivar answered with, "Never! You shall cry the last before I! The curtain of darkness shall hold back the Crimson Tide! So say I, Blackivar the bold and beautiful!"

Rakival suddenly stopped short his pulling and pushing. His intense stare at Blackivar caused the Black Dragon to stop his play acting as well.

"What?" said Blackivar.

Rakival, with obvious disgust in his voice said, "The curtain of darkness? The bold and beautiful? Just a bit sick and soapy, don't you think?"

Blackivar, obviously upset by being verbally dressed down by the red Dragon, retorted with, "What!? You think you're the only Dragon with a flair for the dramatic?"

Rakival returned with, "In a word, yes."

Starting in disgust, Blackivar responded, "In a word, horse hockey!"

To which Rakival said, "That's two words, you midnight colored mental midget!"

So then Blackivar said, "Under all that crimson, you're still pink!"

And Rakival then said, "Back off, you oil slick that talks!"

So Blackivar said, "Pink as bubblegum, and just as soft!"

To which Rakival yelled, "I'll bet you actually went along with all of the weird and perverted stuff that Mathesus wanted you to do, didn't you!?"

And in response, Blackivar yelled a litany of curses that we wont print here.

"You candy coated lizard! You talking jawbreaker with bad breath! You're nothing but an all-day sucker with scales!"

Then Rakival returned with, "Look who is talking about all-day suckers, you-joy toy to a perverted wizard!"

At this, Blackivar wass beginning to seriously lose his cool, when he says, "Joy toy!? I'll show you who's a joy toy after I turn you into cheap luggage and smelly wallets !"

Chapter ELEVEN

Concerned things are getting a bit out of hand, Dibble Dobble attempts to get things back on track by saying, "Oh Great and Terrible Mountains of Attitude. Is there a chance that we can stick to the contest at hand, as it were?"

Both Blackivar and Rakival said together, "Read our fangs, small fry! Shut up!"

Cowering behind the battlements at the edge of the towers top, the small servant muttered more to himself than to anyone else, "Yes, sir's. Thank you, Sirs. Shutting up now, sirs."

Rakival then turned back to face Blackivar and said, "Now! What was I saying before that measly midget on stilts interrupted us?"

Blackivar smiled and said, "You were about to yield to me, you pink pony ride with acid reflux!"

"In a pig's eye!" yelled Rakival. "And in your case, an oiled pig!"

Blackivar rushed forward, getting Rakival in a wrestler's tight hold grip. He says, "I'll show you an oiled pig you pink sows belly!"

To which Rakival yelled, "Don't forget the shaved baboons, you Wizard's winking weasel!"

That last part put Blackivar over the edge. And he yelled, "Oh! You are so done!"

While in the clutch with Rakival, Blackivar grabs one of Rakival's forelimbs. He then spins his black scaled hip into the red Dragon, pulling Rakival across in a judo style throw.

Now this was the first time in written history that a dragon had performed such a move on another Dragon. And since the only witnesses were two dimwitted wizards and a vertically challenged con man, the chances that it would actually become part of recorded history were slim to nil.

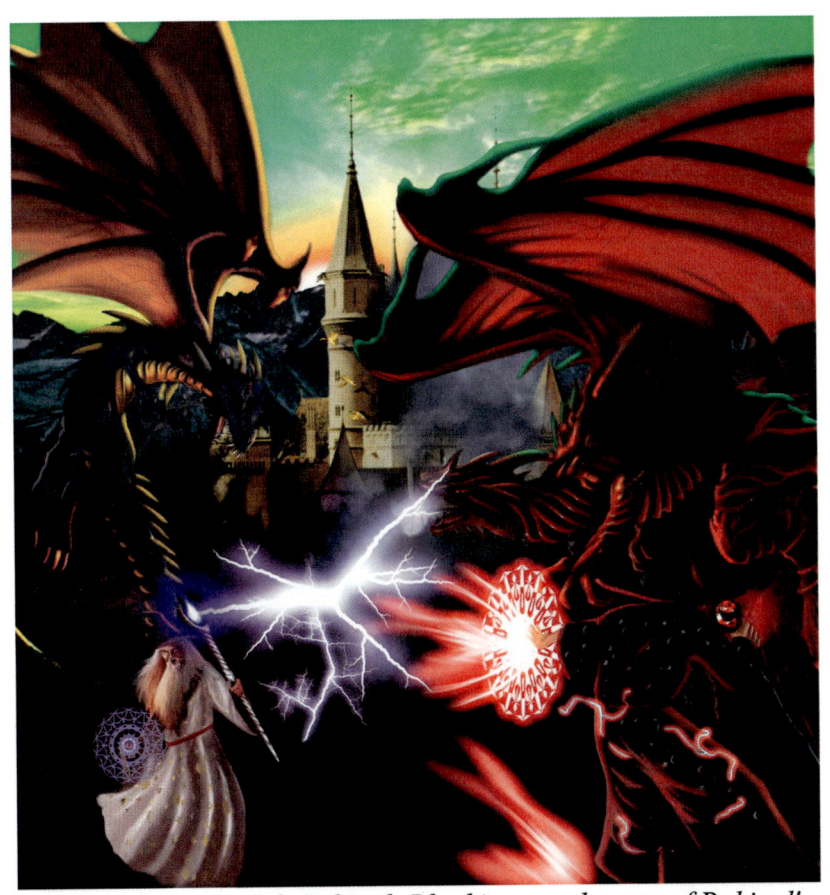

The Worrisome War of the Whimsical Wizards   NM Reed & WL Preston

"While in the clutch with Rakival, Blackivar grabs one of Rakival's forelimbs. He then spins his black scaled hip into the red Dragon, pulling Rakival across in a judo style throw."

Rakival was taken totally by surprise by the move, sailing through the air with a wide-eyed look on his blood red face. Thanks to Blackivar's incredible strength and Rakival's incredible size, the red Dragon hit the ground of the Blasted Plain hard.

Very hard. This impact caused a local seismic event, also unrecorded in the history of this region, because, well, almost all of the ancient wizards were now dead. And we can see here part of the reason why.

Both wizards were thrown to the ground, causing Bartimon to spill his stuffies from his 'CROW ROYA' bag.

Mathesus Loton managed to put a sizable dent in his magic bedpan, which the magic item did not appreciate one little bit.

The already teetering Tower of Observance was sent over beyond the point of no return. It toppled over and landed with a crushing effect on Blackivar's tail. The Black Dragon howled in pain, spinning and thrashing about from the injury to his scaly pride.

The fall of the tower, and its resulting crash across the Dragon's tail, threw Dibble Dobble a great distance across the Blasted Plain. Fortunately for him, but unfortunately for Bartimon's stuffies, the short servant's landing was cushioned by the animated heap of toys. Several were smashed flat, never to rise again. Another karmic moment scored against the stuffies by Dibble Dobble.

As soon as he was able to rise, Dibble Dobble ran away as fast as his stilted legs could carry him. The surviving stuffies gave chase, intent on evening the score for their lost members. Seeing that he was being pursued by a plush lynch mob, the short servant succeeded in setting an unofficial land speed record on stilts. And he quickly left the Blasted Plain behind.

The Worrisome War of the Whimsical Wizards   NM Reed & WL Preston

The Worrisome War of the Whimsical Wizards

NM Reed & WL Preston

The Worrisome War of the Whimsical Wizards					NM Reed & WL Preston

Chapter TWELVE

Bartimon, seeing who he still thought was that Wizarding Herald leaving the dueling Plain at high speed, pursued by many of his stuffies, decided to beat a quick retreat as well.

Given all of the action that was still going on between the black and the red dragons, elsewhere was obviously safer than this place.

Bartimon quickly gathered up the smashed stuffies from the ground, putting them in his 'CROW ROYA' bag. When the last went in, he spotted something that must have been dropped by the Wizarding Herald.

A curious mask.

Bartimon thought it looked familiar, but at the moment, he could not bring to mind where he had seen it before. Casting a glance at the still fighting dragons, he quickly tossed it in his 'CROW ROYA' bag, put the bag over his shoulder, and beat feet in the direction of the rest of his stuffies.

Perhaps, he thought, *the wizarding herald can explain where this mask came from. I had better catch up before my plushy friends beat him to a pulp.*

Mathesus Loton, still back on the Blasted Plain, decided he might stay around and watch the outcome of the battle royale between the two dragons. Rakival had just succeeded in returning Blackivar's favor of low-level orbit flight, by throwing the Black Dragon a goodly distance across the Blasted Plain. The impact tossed Mathesus to the ground once again, spilling his magic bedpan from its place in his robes. The magic item, aware of its imminent demise in this place of great danger, decided to abandon its creator to his fate. It levitated off the ash covered ground, then flew off in the direction everyone else had taken at high speed.

Mathesus cursed magic bedpan as it left him behind. Looking about the Blasted Plain, the black clad wizard realized he was the last non-Dragon in the area. And given the fact that the red and black dragons were still heavily involved in the titanic dustup, it dawned on Mathesus that anywhere other than here might be a safer place to be. He could always come back later and find out who had won, and thusly, which wizard had won the dual. After this fight, he figured there would, no doubt, be a dead Dragon laying here.

But at the moment both combatants were alive and kicking. And that translated into a stomping of anyone that got in their way.

And Mathesus decided to summon some swiftly moving servants to carry him away to safety.

Abandoned by his magic boomboom bucket of Rapid Motions, he called up the first thing that entered his twisted brain. After some brief but effective magic mumbo-jumbo, an array of shave-assed baboons appeared around him.

When the simians took stock of the imminent danger of stomping they were likely to get from the dragons, they did the predictable. As a group, the baboons threw a literal shotgun blast of monkey poop at Mathesus Loton. They then hightailed it en masse to the nearby hills for safety. The dark clad wizard, now coated head to foot in baboon bonbons, decided to beat a hasty retreat himself, finally calling back his cauldron to carry him.

The Worrisome War of the Whimsical Wizards — NM Reed & WL Preston

"The dark clad wizard, now coated head to foot in baboon bonbons, decided to beat a hasty retreat himself, finally calling back his cauldron to carry him."

He ended up, after dodging a dragon two step by Rakival, heading in the direction that Dibble Dobble, the stuffies, the bedpan and Bartimon were all going.

This left Rakival the Red Dragon, and Blackivar the Black Dragon, the entire Blasted Plain to work out their differences. And given that full-grown dragons are no pushovers when it comes to events involving massive amounts of destruction, the so-called Blasted Plain ended up looking even worse for wear than before after they were done.

Chapter THIRTEEN

Rakival was the first, after four straight hours of beating, bashing, clawing, biting, spitting, and hurling foul language, to call a brief pause in the destructive festivities.

The Worrisome War of the Whimsical Wizards   NM Reed & WL Preston

"*Rakival was the first, after four straight hours of beating, bashing, clawing, biting, spitting, and hurling foul language, to call a brief pause in the destructive festivities.*"

"Blackivar!" he said. "Hang on a moment!"

Blackivar, staggering at this point, but far from calling it quits, stood his ground. "I plan to hang on a moment. To your head as I twist it off! What are you playing at Rakival?' he said with a sly smile on his scaley and bloody face. "Had enough?"

The red Dragon shook his head in reply, causing some blood, sweat, and a few loose scales to go flying off in random directions. He raised both paws before himself, holding open palms out for Blackivar to see. He then said, "Think about this for a moment. Do you still feel the summoning spell of Mathesus on you?"

Rakival waited for a reply. Blackivar, planning to launch himself yet again at Rakival, paused for a minute to think over the red dragon's words. A moment of realization dawned on the black dragon's mind.

"The spell ran out of power!" said Blackivar. "I am free from that little pervert's commands."

Blackivar then looked intently at Rakival. "And you?" he said. "Has that dim wit Bartimon's spell run out on you?"

Rakival nodded, letting loose a sigh of relief. "We are both free again. No more pointless fighting need come between us. We can call it a draw and walk away. What do you think, Blackivar?"

Blackivar thought it over for a moment, while surveying the wounded state both he and Rakival were in. He took in a deep breath, then coughed it out in a gasp. He obviously had some broken ribs to tend to. And his poor tail needed a month in traction. He decided to choose his next words carefully..

"You know," said Blackivar, "those were some pretty heavy insults you threw at me. You think I can just let that go?"

Rakival sat back on his haunches and raised his

forepaws yet again in a show of peace. He said, "You threw some fairly acid filled comments at me as well. If I can let yours go, you should be able to let mine slide. Besides, would any of this have happened if those two dimwit wizards hadn't summoned us? Both you and I would have been off in our own stomping grounds, doing what we love best. You know, bringing terror to all we see. Now, how are we to go about our daily chores of burning villages, eating livestock by the dozens, and accepting bribes of gold, jewels, and human princesses if we stand around here and kill each other.?"

Rakival paused a moment to let that sink in. Blackivar didn't need much time to see the Rakival was right.

And he said so.

"Rakival the Red. You are a wise Dragon. How could I have lost my cool so completely? This is stupid! What are we doing here? A couple of doofus wizards summon us to compete in a dumb duel. A runt on stilts has us thumb fighting, when we have no thumbs in the first place! Then we play it up, but go too far and turn it into a dragon Donnybrook! How could both of us have gotten so out of control?"

Rakival smiled, revealing to Blackivar that three of his fangs were missing. "Easy," the Red Dragon said. "We are too bad ass dragons with bad attitudes to match. Anyone ever messes with us, and we come down on them and their village like an earthquake."

"And a firestorm!" said Blackivar. "You are so right." The Black Dragon rubbed his left side and winced. "I don't know about you, but I have had enough of this stupid crap."

Rakival rubbed his head and winced as well. "I second that motion. Let us take our wounded backsides from this place, and find greener pastures. I am certain there is a nearby village that needs burning. Or maybe a castle that needs smashing? What do you say?"

Blackivar began walking, limping slightly, beside Rakival as they left the Blasted Plain together. "I say, it shall be a month of Sundays before I feel better. The destruction of a village or three will be very therapeutic. Let's go whip some ass!"

The terror spree on villages that the two dragons had planned never actually happened. Realizing that both of them were really badly wounded, they both decided to head off to their own individual caves to heal up. And given the extent of their injuries, their recovery time was long and drawn out.

And the loyal populaces of all the nearby villages, cities, and castles never realized the bullet they had collectively dodged!

Chapter FOURTEEN

Now, getting back to the wizards and their so-called servant, a rather interesting series of events was about to come into play.

After their exits from the scene of the Dragon dust-up, a rather interesting and comical race was being run.

Dibble Dobble was still trying to outdistance his pursuing group of stuffies. But his surge of adrenaline, brought on by his fall off the tower and his near-death by Dragon stomping, was beginning to wear off.

The short servant was starting to tire, and his strap-on stilts were beginning to feel like lead weights. He glanced back occasionally, seeing that the plush mob was closing the distance. And none of them looked tired in the least.

Just determined.

And they were. The plush bed mates of Bartimon Montinair had gotten it into their collective cotton-stuffed heads to levy a measure of payback against this person of interest. One third of their number had been smashed into useless doilies by this guy on stilts, and the remaining members of the stuffy group were bound and determined to do some doily making themselves.

The Worrisome War of the Whimsical Wizards　　　　　　NM Reed & WL Preston

"Dibble Dobble was still trying to outdistance his pursuing group of stuffies. But his surge of adrenaline, brought on by his fall off the tower and his near-death by Dragon stomping, was beginning to wear off."

And being animated magic items, they had no worries about getting tired. They could travel for days like this, and they knew it.

Dibble Dobble was not gifted with such magical endurance, so a meeting between him and the stuffies was inevitable.

Bartimon Montinair, losing sight of, first, the wizardry herald, and then, his stuffy creations, was aware that his age and general physical condition was slowing him in this foot race.

Determined to catch up with those he pursued, the paisley bedecked wizard stopped trotting. He took his 'CROW ROYA' magic bag of purple velvet from off his shoulder, and placed it on the ground. Taking the yellow gold tie chords of the bag in each hand, Bartimon opened the bag at his feet. He then stepped into the bag, bringing the mouth of the purple sack up to his waist level and tied it securely to hold it on.

He uttered the magic words "Sack Race", and the magic 'CROW ROYA' bag began hopping along at a steady pace, carrying Bartimon Montinair with it.

By sight and by twisting to the right or to the left, the wizard was able to guide his magical conveyance along. By ushering the magical words "hare" or "tortoise", the paisley-bedecked wizard was able to hasten or slow down his pace.

By uttering the magic words "hare with its tail on fire", he had managed to get the magic bag up to its highest hopping speed. He felt certain he might catch up to the group ahead before any serious stuffy vengeance could be levied on the wizarding herald.

At least Bartimon hoped so.

The Magic Bedpan was long gone. Trailing Dibble Dobble, the stuffies, and Bartimon, was Mathesus Loton.

Being younger, and loaded with every form of aphrodisiac imaginable, he was making good speed away from the Blasted Plain.

As he moved along, the smell of 'au de simion' began to registering seriously in his nostrils.

"Just my luck," thought Mathesus. "I show up for a date with a curvaceous sorceress who turns out to be a doddering old man. I enter into a duel the turns into a comedy of errors. And now," he sniffs at himself and wrinkled his nose, "I smell like the turd in the punch bowl that has brought an end to the party. I must get back to my hideout in the side of the mountain. Only a long hot oil bath, and my vibrating devices playing the symphony of the angry bee all over my body will put me in a better mood. Perhaps some good beatings on the hide of my servant Dobble will make me happy. Perhaps."

Mathesus continued to trot along, unaware that he was inadvertently following the rest of the party from the Blasted Plain. A few moments later, the dark-cloth and baboon feces-clad wizard began hearing a curious, dull thumping sound that came from somewhere up ahead. Picking up his pace to a run, Mathesus caught sight of Bartimon hopping along in his purple sack.

Hop hop hop went the paisley bedecked wizard, just ahead of Mathesus.

Well, thought the dark and mysterious stinking wizard. *Perhaps my servant will have to wait a bit for his beatings. The first order of business that comes to my mind is pounding the boogers out of that paisley painted pansy! Oh yes!* thought Mathesus. *The final challenge of the dual will be of my choosing! And I choose to beat the snot out of that doddering old fool! Some creative dance steps on his head with my hobnailed boots should definitely leave a dull impression on his mind!*

Mathesus Loton broke into a flat-out run, flinging

baboon bonbons in random directions as he went. He quickly began to close the distance on his prey.
    And so the race continued for a short time thereafter.....
    Until…..

Chapter FIFTEEN

Dibble Dobble, in the lead, was just about to call it quits, when the stuffies, in a sudden burst of speed, overtook him. They slammed him to the ground, and proceeded to perform a dance called "mob violence" all over his body.

Bartimon Montinair was a-hop hop hopping along, only to find that he was about to land directly on top of the pile of stuffies and the object of their brutal affections.

He quickly uttered the words, "On a dime and leave six cents change!" This caused the magic 'CROW ROYA' bag to stop just short of the pile of battling forms.

But then, in a flying leap with a tackle from behind, Mathesus Loton grabbed and drove Bartimon Montinair into the heap of butt-kicking on the ground.

Thus total pandemonium erupted.

Another number of the stuffies got smashed into useless hand rags by the impact of the magic purple bag of Bartimon. A few others ended their days as doormats under the metal-shod biker boots of Mathesus.

And under it all, Dibble Dobble was becoming one with architecture. He was getting first-hand knowledge of what it feels like to be the base of a pillar. Or rather, the smashed and flattened dirt underneath it.

A few stuffies that remained 'alive' turned their violent attentions on Mathesus Loton. With his lead-shot-filled gloves, the dark clad wizard made short work of Bartimon's bed buddies.

The Paisley clad wizard was slapping ineffectively at Mathesus, attempting to stop this wholesale destruction of his cloth-bodied friends.

Dibble Dobble, pinned under the weight of Bartimon and his magic purple bag, could only groan in an attempt to take in short gasps of life-giving air.

Once the stuffies were all dispatched, Mathesus

Loton turned his attentions back to his intended prey. He grabbed Bartimon by the shoulder with his left hand, and squeezed the old man's flesh and bones like a vice. Mathesus then drew back his right fist and cocked it like a pistol hammer.

"Any last words, you total hemorrhoid on my sphincter?" he said.

Bartimon, desperate to defend himself from imminent destruction grabbed the only thing available from his purple bag and held it before his face.

The curious mask he had found on the Blasted Plain.

"Please!" cried Bartimon. "I am allergic to pain! I break out in bumps and bruises! Mercy, fellow wizard! Mercy!"

Mathesus Loton never delivered the skull smashing blow he had intended to gift Bartimon with. He released the older wizard, and with both of his gloved hands, Mathesus took hold of the mask.

Bartimon, uncertain of what to expect, let go of the mask, but kept both of his eyes firmly closed. He did not want to see it coming..

A moment of silence followed, punctuated only by the occasional gasps for breath by Dibble Dobble on the ground.

Bartimon slowly opened one eye, then the other. He looked at Mathesus Loton, whose whole attention was focused on the curious mask.

Mathesus finally snapped out of his momentary daze. He looked up from studying the mask, and focused his attention on Bartimon Montinair.

"Where?" he asked, "did you get this mask? Do you know who this belongs to?" The dark clad wizard turned the face-covering item around so that Bartimon might see it better.

Then it hit him like a ton of adobe bricks. The old

wizard had seen this face mask before! On the face of his servant.

"Dibble?!" He said.

"Dobble?!" cried Mathesus in obvious rage.

"Uh, oh..." muttered the small servant from his place on the ground.

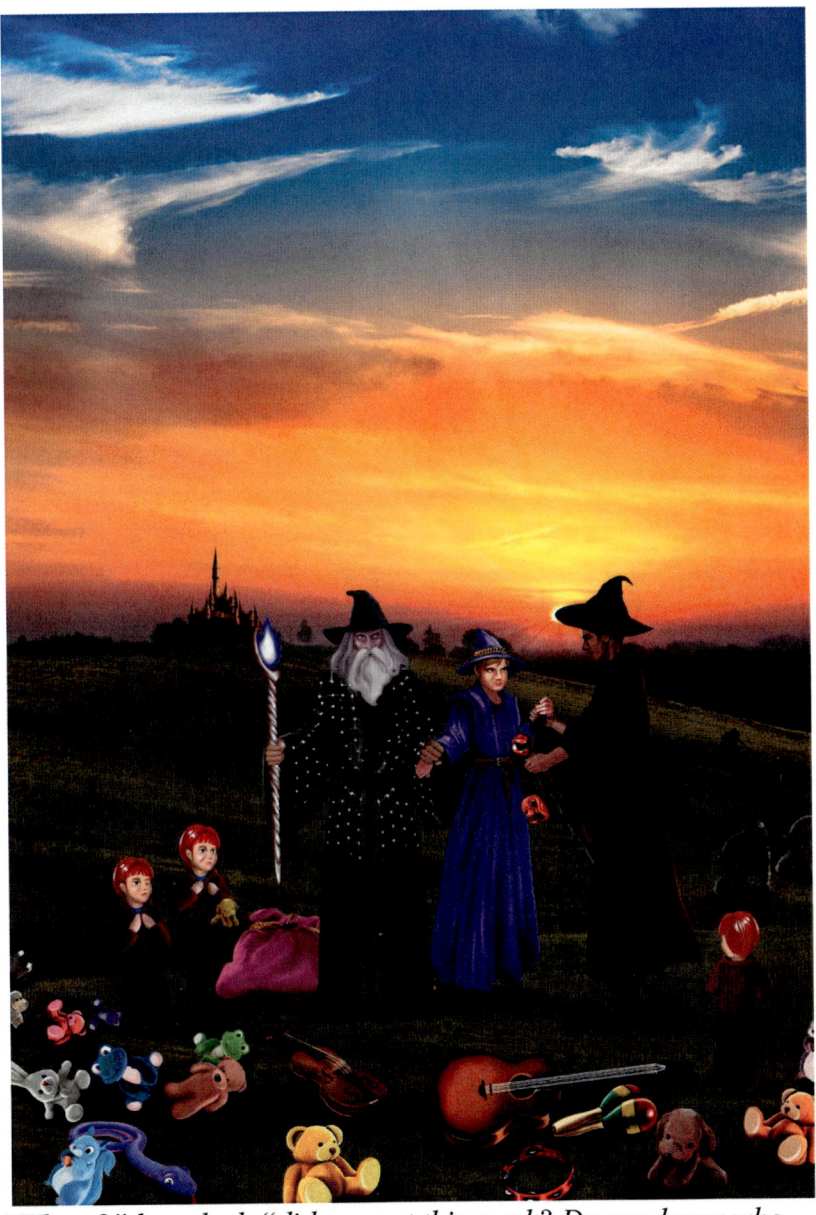

The Worrisome War of the Whimsical Wizards   NM Reed & WL Preston

" "Where?" he asked, "did you get this mask? Do you know who this belongs to?" The dark clad wizard turned the face-covering item around so that Bartimon might see it better.   Then it hit him like a ton of adobe bricks. The old wizard had seen this face mask before! On the face of his servant.   "Dibble?!" He said. "Dobble?!" cried Mathesus in obvious rage.   "Uh, oh..." muttered the small servant from his place on the ground. "

Both wizards turned their attentions to the stilt-wearing runt with the stuffy-mutilated robes, who currently occupied a patch of ground under Bartimon and his purple bag. The paisley bedecked wizard slowly stepped out of his 'CROW ROYA' bag thus relieving Dibble Dobble of a terrible pain in his spine, pelvic region, colon, and kidneys. Bartimon then lifted his purple sack up off the small servant, and held it open to one side. He then looked to Mathesus Loton, indicated the live lump on the ground with his free hand, and said, pointing to the opening in the bag, "if you wouldn't mind?"

"Gladly," said Mathesus, as he grabbed Dibble Dobble by the stilts and hoisted him high in the air. Even from his inverted perspective, the small servant could see from the mutual looks of displeasure on the faces of both wizards, that the fecal material had indeed hit the rotary oscillator.

Or, more simply put, the proverbial doodoo head hit the fan.

"Well, runt?" said Mathesus, nose to nose with Dibble Dobble. "Anything to say before we pass judgment on you? I can assure you, this is going to hurt you far worse than anything you might have suffered before!"

The small servant's nose was already suffering in torment as it was assailed by the combined odors of Bartimon's sachet and peppermint breath candies, and Mathesus' combination of heavily garlicked breath, cheap cologne, B. 0., heavy metal, sweaty leather, and spicy monkey crap.

And Dibble Dobble's eyes began to tear up as though he had been a happy recipient of a pepper spray facial treatment.

"Umm...." He finally managed, to say. ".... Well... ... You see... ... I was just... ... Well... ... Here's the thing... ... I... ...uhmm..."

Dibble Dobble looked to kind hearted Bartimon Montinair for a possible suspension of sentence. But the older wizard was slowly shaking his head in a negative manner saying, "Dibble, this level of naughtiness goes beyond anything I have ever suffered from by serving staff. I am afraid that Mathesus Loton and I will have to think up some suitable punishment for you. In the meantime....."

Bartimon turned to face Mathesus. When the black clad wizard looked at the older magician, Bartimon indicated the open purple bag. He said, "We can keep this pint-sized criminal in here. And I assure you Mathesus, he shall be secure. And he will have no end of attention given to him by my magical items inside."

Displaying a look of grim determination on his face, Mathesus turned, holding the upside-down servant over the open bag. Bartimon held it open to receive its new occupant, as Mathesus let go of the stilts.

Dibble Dobble fell for a goodly distance within the confines of the magic purple bag.

After what felt like a four-story drop, he landed on a pile of expired stuffies. Looking up to where he had fallen from, Dibble Dobble could see the faces of Mathesus Loton and Bartimon Montinair looking down at him. It looked to the small servant that they were looking down through a hole at the top of a huge purple circus tent. And much to his great regret, he could see that they were both smiling down at him.

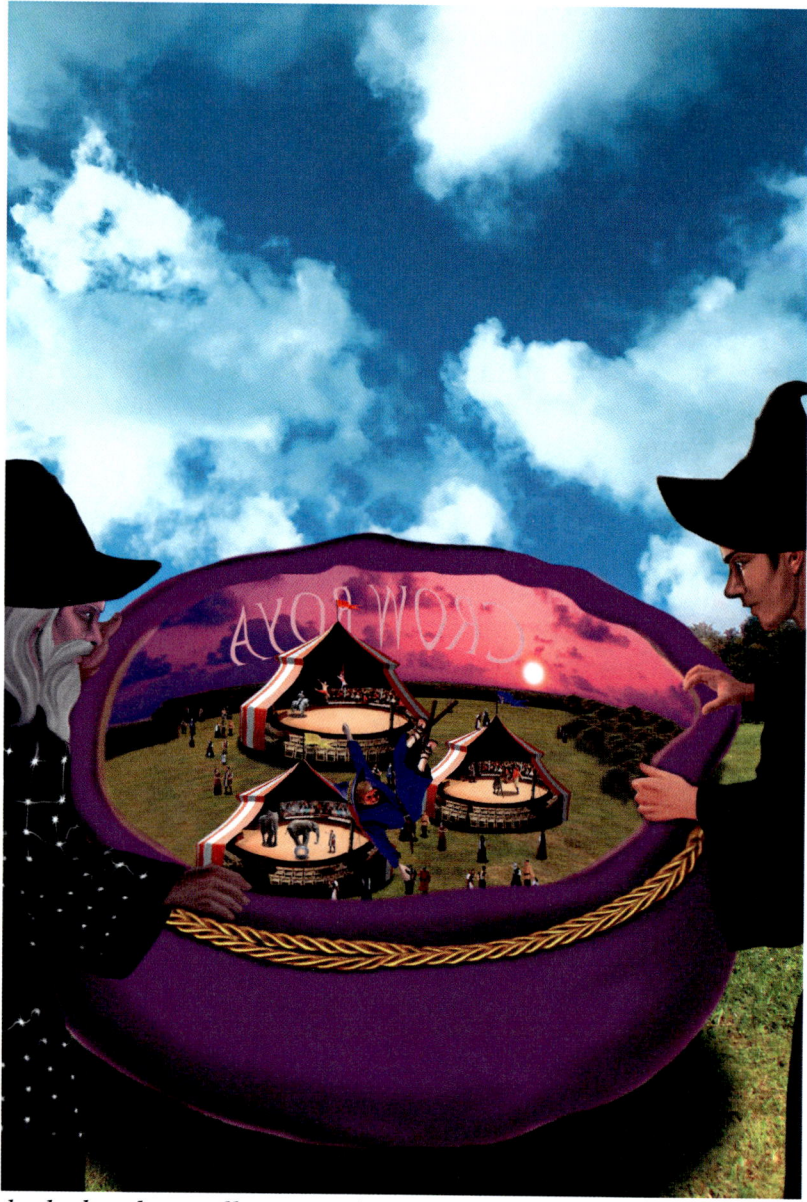

The Worrisome War of the Whimsical Wizards — NM Reed & WL Preston

"It looked to the small servant that they were looking down through a hole at the top of a huge purple circus tent. And much to his great regret, he could see that they were both smiling down at him."

Bartimon said, "And now, for a suitable musical interlude. "The naughty servant bump and grind". Magical instruments! You may begin! And a one, and a two, and a...."

Suddenly, from all around Dibble Dobble, every one of Bartimon's magical musical instruments began playing... ON Dibble Dobble! He was whacked, bumped, pounded, and generally abused from all possible angles.

Above, watching the musical festivities, Mathesus said to Bartimon, "Do you know the Symphony of the Angry Bee?"

To which the older wizard replied, "No, but if you hum a few bars, I can fake it."

Mathesus shook his head, and said, "No, I hate it when they fake it."

The End (for now anyway. The enchanted Chamber Pot is still unavailable for comment.)

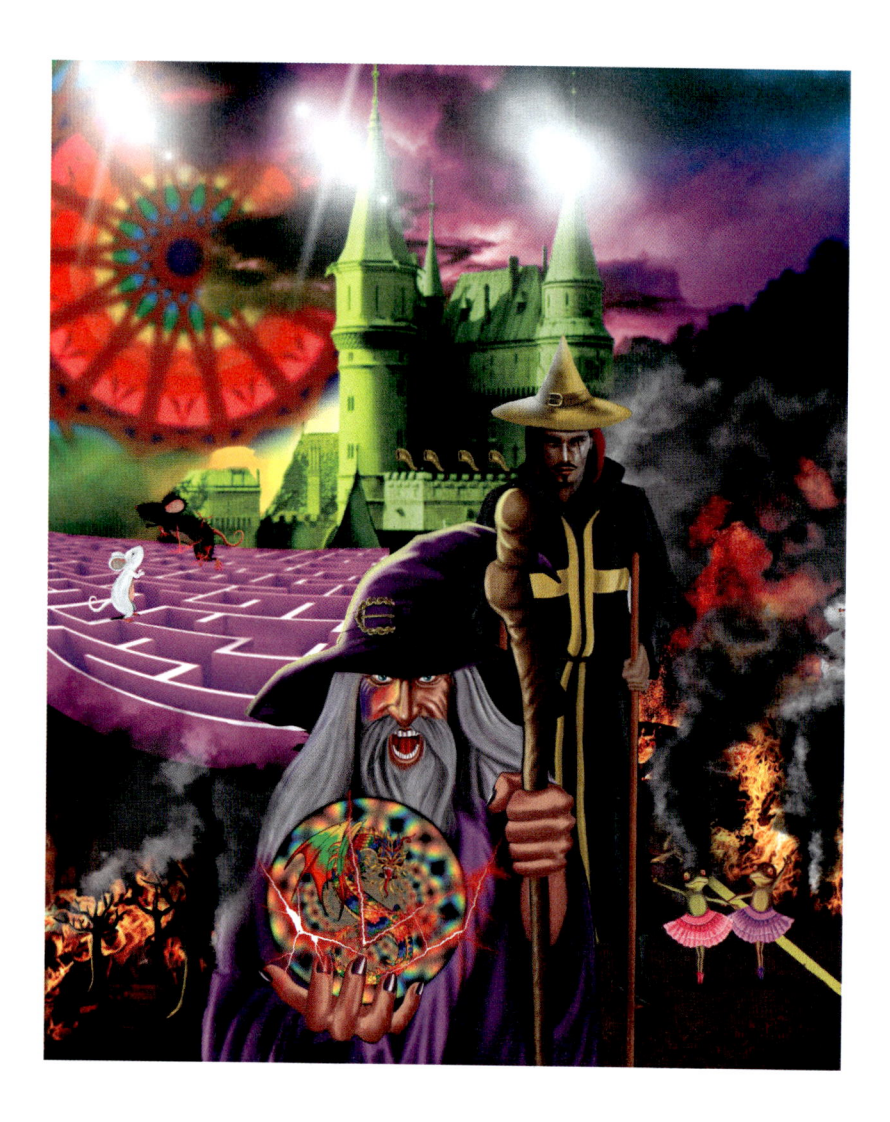

The Worrisome War of the Whimsical Wizards NM Reed & WL Preston

Next up:
The Worrisome War of the Whimsical Wizards Part 2:
Dungeons For Dollars

N. M. Reed and **Whitney Lee Preston** are the dynamic authors of dozens of titles. They live in Northern California on a ranch with lots of animals and books.

Captains Rogue
1. "Belerophon and the Crystal Sphere"
2. "The Rescue of the Galactic Empress and the Lament Cube"
3. "The Green Man Horror"
4. "Starship Revenant"
5. "Death Dust and Planet B"
"Home Is Where the Horse Is: Surviving the Jackson Butte fire disaster 2015"
"After the Fire: Butte Fire Re-population"
"Wind in My Mane: Endurance Ride Stories 1 &2"
"Adventures of Elf and Troll"
"The Saga of Elf and Troll: The Tattered Unicorn"
"The Oak Grove of Maeve"
"Worrisome Wizard War"
"Dungeons For Dollars: Wizard's Hell Cave"

"The Littlest Coyote" and its coloring book
"Romancing the Scroll"
"The Original Origin Story"
"The Glass Planet 1, 2, 3, 4"

and other titles available on:

www.TatteredUnicornPublishing.com

Made in the USA
Columbia, SC
30 November 2022